Neither one of them could sleep.
Maybe it wa

"Can't you sleep?"

"No. You?"

"No."

"I
t
b
s

Duke wrapped his hands around the railing as if he wanted to choke it. "You do disturb me, Beth. I want you." His voice was as deep as the night, and almost as dark. "I want you so damn bad, I'm gritting my teeth to keep from grabbing you right now."

Her mind went blank, but her body hummed in reaction. At last she found her voice. "I thought you said you weren't ready. I thought you really didn't want me."

He turned slowly and stared down at her. "I lied."

Since 1985, Texan **Rita Clay Estrada** has been a favorite with Temptation readers, so when we're looking for special authors to create special projects, her name always comes up. This time we asked her what she could do with a "wrong bed." Find out for yourself in *Love Me, Love My Bed*, Rita's seventeenth Temptation novel.

Books by Rita Clay Estrada

Don't miss any of our special offers. Write to us at the following address for information on our newest releases.

Harlequin Reader Service
U.S.: 3010 Walden Ave., P.O. Box 1325, Buffalo, NY 14269
Canadian: P.O. Box 609, Fort Erie, Ont. L2A 5X3

Rita Clay Estrada
LOVE ME, LOVE MY BED

Harlequin Books

**TORONTO • NEW YORK • LONDON
AMSTERDAM • PARIS • SYDNEY • HAMBURG
STOCKHOLM • ATHENS • TOKYO • MILAN
MADRID • WARSAW • BUDAPEST • AUCKLAND**

For two very important people in my life:
Steve Goodwin, the Stormchaser.
May you find your rainbow—you deserve it.
And for Mary Tate Engles. Thanks for your many years
of friendship and the use of your beautiful Tucson home.

ISBN 0-373-25695-7

LOVE ME, LOVE MY BED

This edition published by arrangement with Harlequin Books S.A.

Printed in U.S.A.

1

IT WAS SOMETHING a handsome sheikh would own to seduce beautiful young maidens, one after another. It was decadent. It was sexy. It was classy but deliciously naughty.

Beth McGruder's new bedroom set was undoubtedly the fulfillment of her fantasy—or at least, half of it. The second half—the man—would probably never arrive. The massive bed had a waist-high frame and four white hand-tooled oak posts connected above by rice-carved poles that served as curtain rods for what had to be hundreds of yards of gauzy white fabric.

And it was all hers.

A giggle caught in her throat, then poured out in tinkling laughter. It was delightfully absurd, owning a bed like this. And the bed didn't stand alone! Oh, no. She'd bought the whole package: a set of small wooden steps that led up to the bed, a table that fit against the foot of the bed, and matching armoires that towered at either side of the massive headboard. In addition to that, she had bought a down-filled comforter, white Battenberg-lace-trimmed sheets and pillow covers, a pleated bed-skirt and several embroidered pillows that would stack nicely with the regular ones.

It was an imposing set that would have looked big even in a barn.

Dropping her purse to the floor and slipping out of her trim black heels, she laughed again. She mounted the miniature ladder-like staircase to the mattress, then crawled to the center of the bed and leaned back against the headboard, her stocking feet stretched straight out in front of her. With a happy sigh, she surveyed the room through the filmy gauze that hung down around her like gossamer mist. Everything looked different.

"The Princess and the Pea," she whispered. And that was how she felt—like a princess.

She'd been divorced for almost three years, living on a shoestring budget for most of that time. It felt very good to have splurged and bought herself the most extravagant bedroom furnishings she could find—and for a price she could afford—barely. The opportunity had just dropped into her lap.

Every day on her way to work as a secretary for Abrams, Abrams and Barrett Law Firm, she'd driven by the furniture store. Glancing at their elaborate displays from the car window had told her that more than likely, anything in the store would be out of her reach financially.

Then, just two months ago, the store began displaying Bankruptcy signs. In the first week the furniture was twenty percent off, then thirty and just last month they'd gone to a forty-percent discount. Beth finally had stopped on her way home one day to look at the remainders. There had been other beds on display, but she hadn't seen beyond this one. It touched the core of her, calling to something she didn't want to delve into or explain, not even to herself.

But even at forty percent off, though, the price of the set was over two thousand dollars, and she couldn't justify the expense. With her heart pounding and her fingers crossed, she told herself that she would come back when the furniture was marked down to fifty percent. Then, if the bed was still there, she would buy it. *If it is still there,* her conscience had taunted. But she'd known she was right to wait. If it wasn't there, then she wasn't meant to have it, she told herself. But her fingers stayed crossed and on the day the signs turned from forty into fifty percent off, she called in to work requesting a personal day off then waited impatiently for the doors to open. When they finally did, she marched in, went directly to the bed and let out a sigh; there was no Sold tag hanging from it yet. But there soon would be.

She took a quick look at her savings passbook and every cent she'd received in the divorce settlement, then wrote a check for the full amount, on the spot.

The saleslady apologized profusely. "I'm sorry, Mrs. McGruder, but we can't deliver for two weeks. We're booked up, and we'll need to wait until we have another delivery going in your direction. After all, this bed will take our people a couple of hours to assemble."

Beth was disappointed, but undaunted. "That's fine. I can wait. After all, I've waited this long."

Later, at home, she had dreamed and anticipated, waiting for delivery. And now it was here—the first new thing she'd bought since the divorce, the first new thing that was just for her.

One more time she gave herself a silent pep talk and told herself she deserved it. After all, a bed was where you spent a third of your life, and from the looks of *her* life at this point, she was going to spend the rest of it single and alone. If that was the case, she would have to catch enjoyment where she could. This would give her pleasure for years to come.

She grinned. It had been the birth of that thought that had allowed her to rationalize purchasing this fantasy without too much guilt in the first place.

"Indulgence." Her voice was as firm as her thoughts were. "Sheer indulgence." The corners of her mouth turned up again. "And well deserved."

The phone rang and she slid from her high perch to the floor, then tried to find her bedroom phone. When she couldn't spot it, she made a mad dash for the cordless in the living room. She answered with a breathless, "Hello?"

"Mrs. McGruder?" asked a deep male voice.

"Yes."

"Did you buy a bed at Simpson's Fine Furniture last week?"

"Yes," she answered slowly, wondering what in heaven's name was going on. Had she entered some kind of contest and they were going to give her a prize? Had she done something wrong? Had her check not cleared? She went through a thousand reasons for the phone call.

"And was it delivered today?"

"Yes." She cleared her throat. "Before I answer any more questions, just who is this?"

"My name is Duke McGregor. I live in the same building as you, in apartment 537, one floor above?"

The name rang a distant bell, but Beth couldn't place it just yet. Instead of saying anything, she waited, and her silence allowed him to continue.

"I bought a bed at Simpson's last week, too. It was a massive, king-size contraption that would take an army of men to install. They said they couldn't deliver it until today, when they delivered yours."

"I see," Beth said. Only she didn't. What did all this have to do with her? "And are you enjoying your new bedroom set, Mr. McGregor?"

"I don't know. Are you?" There was just a hint of teasing—or was it sarcasm?—in his voice.

Was this man a little off his rocker? She pulled the phone away from her ear and stared at it as if it held the answer to her unasked question. She put it back against her ear and asked the least aggressive question she could think of: "I beg your pardon?"

Obviously a patient man, he repeated the question. "I said, I don't know. Are you enjoying my bed, Ms. McGruder?"

"I don't think so," she answered. "Are you hallucinating about your own bed or is this just an obscene phone call in general?"

He gave a heavy sigh—one that told her he was holding on to his patience—barely. "In error, my bed was delivered to your apartment. You haven't noticed, Ms. McGruder, that you have a strange walnut-and-leather bedroom suite in your home?"

This time she stared at the ceiling, hearing a telltale squeak in the floor where he must have been pacing. There it went again. "I'm so sorry, but I think you must have the wrong nut. But I wish you well in your quest, Mr.—" She couldn't remember what his name was.

"McGregor," he supplied with a hint of testiness. "Duke McGregor."

"Duke McGregor," she repeated, then suddenly she remembered where she'd heard the name before. "Are you Benjamin McGregor's father?" she asked.

"Yes. How did you know?"

"My daughters went to school with your son," she finally admitted.

"Your daughters?" he asked slowly, as if piecing together his memories, just as Beth had done a moment ago. "Meaning two?" Then he hesitated. "As in twins?"

"Yes."

"The McGruder twins?"

"Yes."

"You're Mrs. Stan McGruder?" He sounded slightly amazed. She didn't know why. She was perfectly harmless. Duke McGregor, on the other hand, was reputed to have a temper the size of Texas. She wanted nothing whatsoever to do with tempers—especially bad ones—and certainly didn't want to speak to someone who was supposedly without manners.

"My, my, it is a small world, isn't it, Mr. Mc-Gregor?" she said smoothly.

"It certainly is, Mrs. McGruder. And how is Mr. McGruder?" There was just enough smugness in his tone to tell her he was asking for a verification of old information.

"Why, I would assume he and his new bride are doing just fine. And how about Mrs. McGregor? Is she still busy with charities and bridge?"

"She certainly is," he answered, but his voice didn't hold a shade of warmth. In fact, he sounded downright testy. "And I assume you know we divorced a little over two years ago."

"I must have forgotten," she said innocently, noticing that he'd finally stopped pacing over that one weak spot in the floor. Obviously, she'd gotten his full attention.

"I'm sure," he said dryly. "But I don't think that's the question of the day, is it?"

"Really?" She grinned. "And what is?"

"Whether or not you're going to hold my bedroom set ransom."

"Ransom? Now why would I do that?"

"Because, so far, Ms. McGruder, you haven't told me whether or not you *have* my bedroom furniture."

She was tired of the baiting game. "I don't have it. How could I? I only have room for my own, which was delivered and set up this afternoon."

"Then the furniture company was wrong and I'm sorry to have bothered you."

Suddenly, she had a new thought. A heavy feeling began to settle in the pit of her stomach. Beth went to the door of her second bedroom, usually a storage room or a spare when the girls were home. "It's quite all right," she said, stalling him in the conversation as she opened the door. Flipping on the light, she stared into the used-to-be-empty room.

She finally found enough voice to interrupt Duke McGregor's apologies. "Uh, Mr. Duke, uh, McGregor?" she finally managed, stepping into the spare room as if she were walking on eggs. "Is your bed brown leather and dark wood with a canopy?"

"Why, yes—" he began.

But she interrupted him again. "With dark wood armoires on each side?"

This time his voice sounded wary. "Yes."

She peeked up at the canopy. "With mirrors on the ceiling above the bed?"

"And five-inch speakers on either side of the headboard?" His voice sounded hopeful.

She leaned forward and looked at each side until she confirmed what he was describing. "Right."

"Yes, well. It's here in all its glory," she drawled.

"So they *did* deliver it." Satisfaction laced his voice.

"They certainly did," Beth stated flatly, looking at the monstrosity squatting in her spare bedroom.

"If it's not an imposition, may I come see it? Your apartment and mine are the same, so I'd get an idea of how it will look when I have it up here."

"And when do you think that will be?" she asked, eager to get the gaudy thing out of her apartment.

"They told me that once they found it, they could probably get it set up in a few days, but no sooner."

"I'm so sorry," she murmured sincerely.

"So am I. I've already given my son my bed to take to college. He picked it up last night because I thought I'd only be in a hotel one night."

"You spent the night in a hotel?" she asked, surprised.

"Of course. I'm in the middle of an audit. I need all the sleep I can get to keep on top of things. I thought it'd only be for one night."

She recalled that he was a very successful CPA specializing in corporations. A numbers man, her friends used to say.

"My goodness. I'm really sorry. Of course, you can come down and see this, ah...your bed." She walked around the side of the bed, opened an armoire and took a deep breath. It was lined in rich-smelling cedar, which was the only good thing she could say about this ugly set.

"Thanks," he said. "Be there in a few minutes."

After he hung up the phone, Beth imagined him racing to the elevator and rushing to her front door.

When he didn't knock on her door immediately, Beth decided she'd been wrong, shrugged him off and began thinking dinner. Peering into the fridge, she hoped to see something that would whet her appetite. None of the fourteen different frozen dinners did it for her. One foot daintily propped on another, she surveyed the bottom shelves.

Nothing there, either.

She opened the pantry.

A jar of peanut butter, half a sleeve of stale crackers, a giant can of spinach and four small tins of tomato sauce. Nothing tempting.

She picked up the phone and dialed her favorite restaurant down the street. Under her breath, she muttered to her upstairs neighbor, "Too late, buster. You can visit your bed some other time, because I'm about to eat dinner. And I dine by candlelight. Alone."

The restaurant answered and she ordered spaghetti, chunky sauce and mozzarella garlic bread for delivery. It felt good to splurge on dinner once in a while, and tonight was a night for celebration. She needed to mark the addition of her new bed to the eclectic family of new and used furniture she'd acquired over the past few years.

It hadn't been easy making the transition from being a married woman living in a spacious home on the golf course in the "right" neighborhood—where she'd raised her children, worked on charities and school boards and taken golf and tennis lessons—to being a single woman who had to work for a living to make ends meet—and they definitely weren't the same ends she'd been used to.

There remained in her a residue of bitterness over the fact that her ex-husband still had money to burn on his new wife. Apparently Stan had no problem funding his mate's manicures, hairdresser bills, extravagant hobbies and clothing. He hadn't been that way with Beth. He hadn't been generous with her— neither with gentle words nor deeds. But rumor had it he had learned a lot between wife number one and wife number two. Number two definitely had his attention.

It was a shame he hadn't learned that lesson before. But that was another story. He *hadn't* learned his lesson and they *had* gotten divorced.

The phone rang and she reached for it, thinking it would be Mr. McGregor apologizing for being late. To her pleasant surprise it was her daughter Carol.

"Hi, honey. What's up?" Beth asked, knowing there wasn't any such thing as a phone call without a purpose from a college girl.

"I need you to find my maroon wool suit and send it to me. Could you, Mom?" The quieter of the twins, Carol was also the more direct. Ask a question, get an answer. "I'm invited to a sorority tea next week and it's perfect for the occasion."

"Fine. I'll mail it from the office tomorrow," Beth promised. "Is everything else okay?"

"Great. Cassandra got eighty-eight on her English test and I made ninety." Carol laughed. "Cass didn't know she was that good until she made two points less than I did."

"Did you study together?" The girls did most everything together, but if they didn't, it was usually because Carol needed more space. Cassandra wouldn't give room without being asked.

"Of course," Carol replied, then asked, "Did you get that bedroom set, yet?"

"It came today," Beth confirmed, emptying the dishwasher as she spoke. "It's absolutely beautiful and I'm so excited I may hit the sheets by seven o'clock, just for the heck of it."

"We can't wait to see it. Are you going to let us sleep in it when we come home?"

Beth laughed. "No way. You're both going to have to blow up those mattresses and sleep on the floor in the spare room. But if you're good, I'll let you watch Letterman with me."

"Anybody else in your life sharing that monstrosity?" Carol asked.

"Don't get smart, young lady. And if that's your *subtle* way of asking if I'm dating someone, the answer is no." Beth wiped the kitchen sink with a sponge.

"I didn't think so, but I know Cass will ask me, so I thought I'd get the right answer in advance."

They spoke for a few more minutes, then Beth hung up, a smile still on her lips. She missed the girls. Raising twins hadn't been easy, but it had always been fun. She was proud of her work as a parent, proud of the way the girls had grown up. And now that they were at University of Texas, she couldn't deny that they were, indeed, grown-up.

One thing hadn't changed, though, and that was their fear of her remarrying. It was all right for their father to do so, but not for her. She was to remain their mother, first and foremost.

Of course, it wasn't a problem because she wasn't marrying. She wasn't even dating, anymore.

She'd tried dating last year, after having waited way over twelve months before sticking her nose out the door to see if there was life after divorce. During that reclusive time, her friends had badgered her to death to get out and meet someone. A few had hinted that what she really needed was an affair. One or two were even more blunt. "Go out and get yourself a man who can take you to bed and calm your nerves a little. It won't hurt and it might help ease that tense look around your mouth!"

Beth had finally taken that advice—once—and decided it just wasn't worth the effort. The few dates she'd had usually involved more than she was ready to deliver, or a man who had war stories of his own, and she didn't want to swap. She was too private for that, and shy. So far, there hadn't been anyone who interested her enough to get through those first several dates it would take to find the jewel of a man.

Instead, she played tennis with her old friends, saw movies with a few of her new acquaintances, and worked with some nice and easy co-workers. That kept her busy enough socially that she didn't have to worry about taking a man to her bed. As far as she was concerned, she could be single for the rest of her life and die content.

It didn't sound great to the average woman, but then Beth found lots of things far more exciting and interesting these days than romance. Having gone from her parents' somber home to her husband's, this was the first time she'd ever been responsible for herself alone. There were so many things she'd wanted to do that she hadn't been able to do before, but now she had the chance, even if it meant doing those things alone. Perhaps this was part of growing—not growing up, but growing wiser.

Enough philosophy, she told herself and went back into her bedroom, and into her fantasy. It took ten minutes to make up the bed. She piled the last pillow in place and began to walk backward to the door so she could get the full effect.

It looked exactly as she'd imagined it—soft, feminine and very, very sensuous. A room designed for dreams—or for lovemaking.

When knocking echoed through the apartment, she reluctantly left to open the front door. She found herself staring into the darkest blue eyes she'd ever seen.

"Beth?" he asked, the corners of his mouth turning up in a breathlessly sexy smile. He held out his hand. "I'm Duke, the owner of the bed in your spare room." His gaze narrowed as he searched her face for... something. "I think we've met before, but I don't remember where."

Beth, her hand resting warmly in his, had to remind herself that it wasn't polite to stare. He was still dressed for work in a black-and-gray striped suit with a red-and-black power tie. He looked sophisticated and successful. She cleared her throat and found her voice. "I'm sure that's true, but don't look to my memory for confirmation."

That wasn't quite honest. She'd actually found the memory, but didn't recall his smile having had such a devastating effect on her libido. It probably wasn't him, though; more likely it was her recent solitary lifestyle that accounted for her reaction.

He frowned. "Perhaps it was the club," he said, referring to the country club where she could no longer afford the dues.

She decided to put him out of his misery. "Perhaps the swim team several years back? I believe your son was on the same team as my girls."

"Really?" His eyes widened as if he'd finally connected her to one of his own memories.

His gaze drifted lazily down the length of her body and then back to her face as slow recognition registered in his blue eyes. Beth wasn't sure, but she sensed he was remembering something she wasn't.

Whatever it was, Duke McGregor apparently wasn't going to dwell on it, because the look was quickly replaced by that sexy smile of his. "I think I remember now," he said. "Your husband coached soccer one year, didn't he?"

She corrected that misconception immediately. "My then-husband supported the coach by doing some of the paperwork. The coach didn't have a computer at the time, and we did." Beth had a memory or two herself. One of those memories had to do with playing three-table bridge with his former wife a few years ago. It had been more a social thing to do through the club than the cutthroat game most knew. She tilted her head and stared up at him. Funny... All through the games, his wife had done nothing but gripe about him and his rip-roaring temper. Tempers and Beth never matched; she ran at the sight of one. But a look into his eyes didn't seem to reveal a hint of that rage. Strange how people hid their problem areas so well....

"Been divorced long?" he asked.

"Long enough to know it was the right choice." She hadn't meant to sound so curt.

"I'm sorry," he murmured, as if he meant it and cared.

"I'm not." She smiled to soften her words. "To quote a friend of mine, 'It's better to have loved and lost, than live with him for the rest of your life.'"

Duke's eyes widened, then he laughed, a deep rumbling laugh that had Beth tingling all the way down to her toes. Oddly, she felt proud of bringing his laughter out, as if she'd achieved something.

The door across the corridor opened and Mrs. Rutgar, Beth's neighbor—a retired piano teacher and widow—peeped out the narrow opening of her chained door. "Are you all right, dearie?" she called.

"I'm fine Mrs. Rutgar. Mr. McGregor lives upstairs. We were just talking."

"Well, all right," the older woman finally said as she eyed Duke McGregor distrustfully. "Call if you need me."

"I will, Mrs. Rutgar," she said reassuringly.

The door slowly closed, then the lock snapped in place like a period at the end of an unspoken opinion.

Reminded of where they were standing, and that the hallway was no place for a private conversation, Beth opened the door to her apartment wider. "I'm sorry. I didn't mean for you to stand out there wondering about the fate of your investment. Please, come in."

"Thanks." He looked relieved.

Duke stepped inside her living room and she could tell he noticed everything about his surroundings. She knew the upholstered furniture was sadly dated, the remnants of a crumbling marriage. But her favorite antiques were also scattered here and there, creating a coziness she loved and needed to feed her soul. The slightly shabby couch and chair reminded her of raising her daughters and of the home she'd tried to build for her family. That was both good and bad, but it was all hers. She tilted her chin as if to defend her life-style.

"I bet you'd like to see your bedroom furniture, wouldn't you?" she asked, diverting his focus from her living room.

"Will you show me yours if I show you mine?" His dark, riveting gaze swung back to her, a slow smile lighting the blue depths. He turned toward her and seemed to suck all the oxygen out of the room, leaving her breathless.

"I'm sure you've seen both in some form or fashion," she said, her face completely deadpan. No man—even one with deep blue eyes and an irresistible smile—was going to win her over and then act so damn *intimate* without her permission!

Duke got the message. He backed off a step and raised his hands in surrender. "I'm sorry. That was completely uncalled for," he apologized. "I was just teasing. It's a little awkward to have a stranger see my choice in bedroom furniture."

Beth went to the bedroom door and turned the knob; he followed close behind. She could almost feel his breath on her nape. She tried for a nonchalance she didn't have. "I don't blame you, Mr. McGregor. There's something unquestionably intimate about a bed, isn't there?" She allowed the door to swing open as she flipped on the light switch.

Duke's eyes widened as he took in the length and breadth of the bed that occupied all but a few feet of her spare bedroom.

A low whistle escaped his lips.

Beth felt vindicated. Even *he* thought the thing looked like someone's nightmare. She smiled. "What do you think?" she asked, already knowing the answer. "It's a piece of work, isn't it?"

"It certainly is," Duke McGregor finally said as he stepped into the room. He tilted his head and looked up at the smoked-mirrored ceiling above the king-size bed. "Isn't it great?"

Beth stared at him in awe and wonder.

There was no accounting for the bad taste of a man who passed for normal and handsome. If this bed looked great to him, she could just imagine the rest of his apartment.

But then she recalled an image of Duke McGregor—something his ex-wife had said several years ago at a neighborhood bridge get-together. While Duke's wife was taking a trick that made her eligible for the deuce prize, she had calmly pronounced that her husband was a sex maniac.

One look at the atrocious bed in front of her, and Beth believed it.

2

DUKE TURNED TO HER and was about to speak when the doorbell rang. *Saved by the bell,* he thought. One look at her wide, hazel eyes and he'd forgotten what he was about to say. She touched his arm lightly and turned, excusing herself as she answered the door.

Beth McGruder was the most sensuous woman he'd ever seen. Her every movement was fluid and rich, her voice was soft and deep and thick, instantly creating sexual images in the back of his mind.

He'd needed the break from her presence. His heart was pumping blood through his body at breakneck speed. He took a deep breath, then turned toward the living room and the person at the door.

A young man with a scraggly scrap of hair on his chin handed Beth two cardboard containers that smelled heavenly, reminding him that he hadn't eaten dinner yet. He hadn't stopped for lunch, either.

When Beth closed the door and headed toward the kitchen with her delivery, her eyes glowed bright with anticipation. "Excuse me," she murmured, "but I've been waiting for this." She flashed a grin that lit up the room. "It's my favorite dinner, you see."

He followed her movement, his eyes locked on her hips, swaying from side to side. "It smells delicious. What is it?"

"Pasta marinara from a little Italian restaurant on Louetta." She set the boxes on the bar and opened one. The aroma that wafted through the kitchen slammed into Duke's senses.

He took another deep breath, smelling the sumptuous marinara sauce. "Smells wonderful."

Her eyes darted up to his, a note of concern shining there. "You haven't eaten yet, either, have you?"

He conjured up a smile. "I was in a hurry to get home to see my new bedroom set."

She hesitated only a moment. "Would you like to share this? They send enough for two, so there's plenty."

He wanted to say yes immediately, but realized it wasn't the correct thing to do. "That's okay. I've got a can of soup with my name on it."

"Just what every growing boy needs," Beth said, pulling out a pot. She filled it with water, then put it on the stove. "Is that what your son eats for dinner?"

"I wish. No, he downs pizzas as if they're growth hormones, and he's grown three inches in less than a year."

"And you?" she asked. "What do you usually eat for dinner when you're home?"

"I told you. Soup."

She made an odd but definitely judgmental sound. "That's not enough to keep a bird alive. Especially tonight, when I already feel guilty because of the error in your delivery."

He was surprised by her words. Was she kidding? No one had felt guilty about him since he'd been a kid and his overprotective mother was watching over his shoulder constantly. "Guilty? Why would you feel guilty? You didn't do anything wrong."

"I didn't have anything to do with your mistaken delivery, but your personal property is still in my spare bedroom." She salted the water and began fussing with dishes, pulling out two sets of everything.

Duke let her. He was tired, hot, and frustrated that his bed wasn't in his apartment where it was supposed to be. Now he was going to have to make other plans for the night. It was one more thing gone wrong in a day of things gone wrong. Because this was personal made it more than the usual frustration.

"Sit on the stool," she ordered gently, pouring red wine into an etched crystal glass and setting it on the counter between them.

Giving in to his original urge, he edged up on the padded stool and heaved a sigh. Having her feed him might be an imposition, but it was right for the time. He was too damn tired to care. "Thanks."

Her impish grin was sexy enough to stir him—but just barely. "You're welcome."

"What are you putting together?" he asked as he watched her peel an elephant clove of garlic.

"I'm adding a few things to my delivered dinner. The restaurant gives so much in their order, I usually have enough for two nights. I'll just have to add a little extra pasta to make it dinner for two."

"Do you do this often?"

"What? Stretch a meal? Of course." She laughed ruefully. "I used to be an expert at this when the kids were young."

"I meant, do you often invite strange men in for dinner?"

She cocked her head to the side and thought for a moment. Then she smiled. "Nope. First time."

Duke picked up his glass and gave her a salute. "May I tell you how glad I am?"

"May I tell you how sorry I am?" she teased as she lifted her glass in answer to his toast. "Occasionally it would have been nice to have company."

"I guess so." He laughed, but he was happy that there hadn't been someone before him; and then he brushed aside the selfish thought. He was more tired than he'd realized if he was harboring pride in being told he was the first man this woman had stretched dinner for since her divorce.

In a few minutes she was serving a plate of spaghetti that taunted his voracious hunger.

The time passed quickly. Good food, good wine, and conversation that seemed to be as comfortable as a favorite pair of bedroom slippers, made for a delightful and much-needed quiet evening.

Duke passed off those feelings, pushing them away without looking at them too closely. He didn't need to analyze every feeling. His ex-wife had done enough of that for him. Instead, he listened to Beth talk about the people in the building, the various businesses along the main highway that had come and gone, and those that had lasted. They talked about buying new bedroom furniture and why now.

"So this is my first big buy since the divorce," she told him, just as he ate the last bite of his spaghetti. The empty plate surprised him; he didn't remember eating so much so quickly. Beth continued, "Until this buy, I've kept all the money from the settlement in a mutual fund. Been afraid to spend it because I knew the girls were heading to college and I had promised to help pay half their expenses the first two years."

"Do you like your choice?"

She didn't hesitate a minute. "I love it."

"I didn't ask properly earlier. May I see it?"

He wasn't sure what he said to bring it on, but he was positive that Beth blushed. "It may not fit everyone's idea of a perfect bedroom set."

She was hedging, but he wasn't sure why. He tried to calm her nerves with his own admission. "I'm sure mine doesn't, either, but I like it."

Reaching for his plate, she stacked it with her own and placed them both in the sink. Her cheeks were tinted a faint pink. Finally, she shrugged, looking everywhere but at him. "Why not?"

With reluctant steps she led him to her bedroom and slowly opened the door. After a heartfelt sigh, she flipped on the light.

Duke's smile slipped off his face as he stared into the room. Breath caught somewhere in his inactive lungs. His feet felt as if they were planted in the carpet, growing roots.

All this room needed was a camel outside the door and burning candles on every surface. To complete the fantasy, he would need a sheet over his shoulder and a white scarf on his head. And he would need her— in the bed—looking both reluctant and excited by the prospect of sharing the expansive mattress with him.

He grinned. The grin turned to laughter.

"I didn't make fun of yours." Her voice was tight and straitlaced. So prim and proper. But now he knew better. This room spoke of another part of Beth McGruder—a secret part.

"You didn't have to. But this is straight out of a fantasy. A *woman's* fantasy."

"Well, I should *hope* so," she said, exasperation lacing her voice. "Last time I looked, that's what I was."

He finally tore his gaze from the sexy bed and looked down at her with a new interest and slight awe. There was obviously more to this woman than he'd realized. "If this bed is any indication, you're certainly all woman."

"Don't be a chauvinist," she stated, crossing her arms over her chest, emphasizing her delicious cleavage. But her eyes shot arrows dipped in poison. "And I certainly *could* have made fun of that monstrosity in the next room."

"That's not a monstrosity. That's a man's idea of a bedroom. Unlike this, this..." His arm swept the room as he tried to think of a word he could use that wouldn't make her more angry with him than she already was. "This fantasy world."

"And yours doesn't have a thing to do with fantasy? A *man's* fantasy of seduction?"

"Well, I..."

He wasn't thinking straight at the moment. He couldn't even come up with an argument. The truth was, she was right. He'd bought a bed that looked as if it belonged in the sixties, in the era of free love and swinging singles. It looked like something his bachelor Uncle Jake, a man he had idolized, would have had in his sophisticated "pad." Duke's first glimpse of his hero's apartment had stayed with him for life. Hence the bed. What was the harm? It was a better release than some.

"Never mind." She uncrossed her arms and stepped back. "It doesn't really matter."

"What do you mean, it doesn't matter? Of course, it matters! It's in your house and it should be in my house. How do I know you don't secretly covet it?"

She walked back into the kitchen, and he followed her; her shoulders shrugged, her hips swayed from side to side delightfully. "It's not my style," she said over her shoulder as she busied herself loading the dishwasher. "It's just too . . . masculine."

Beth bent over the dishwasher door and sprinkled soap powder into the holder. Then, with swift, clean motions, she closed the door, flipped the switch and turned to face him, her back to the machine she'd just loaded.

Her chin was tilted at a determined angle that made Duke want to grin. He did just that.

Beth smiled back. "And you love that tasteless pile of wood and glass."

He started to protest, then decided against it. "Yes."

She chuckled and he joined in. It was a relief. He hadn't laughed in a long time. Oh, he'd given the polite laugh after a bad joke or a funny expression from one of his workers, but he hadn't felt the deep belly laugh that comes from pure and total enjoyment of a moment in time.

The silence they finally allowed in was louder than the laughter. He stared down at her, amazed that he was still here and nothing about his bed had been resolved.

Duke cleared his throat. "I need to make arrangements to get that pile of wood and glass out of your bedroom and into mine."

"I understand. You said it would be a few days?"

"Not anymore. When I called the furniture company to tell them I'd found the bed, they told me there was a waiting list and I'd have to go to the end of it."

"Goodness!" Beth looked startled. "It took so long to get it in the first place!"

He tried to look sad. "I know. I guess I'll just have to visit it in the evening before I leave for the hotel, where I'll be sleeping for the next two weeks."

"You can't get it moved before then?"

"Not without spending *another* fortune."

Beth flipped on the coffee-making machine and with swift, economic movements began making cappuccino. Duke loved cappuccino, but he'd never learned how to operate the machine when he was married, and he certainly wasn't about to start, now that he was alone.

A few minutes later, she'd led him back into the living room area and handed him a cup as well as tongs for a brown sugar cube. He took one and stirred thoughtfully for a moment before speaking. He had a solution to his dilemma, and maybe it would help her out, too. All he had to do was find the right way to approach her.

"Duke," Beth murmured slowly. "There is one solution we haven't touched on." She looked up at him, her eyes wide and forest green. "We could try something else and see if it works. You know, like on a trial basis?"

He hoped it was the same way he was thinking. "What?"

His forehead wrinkled into a frown as she chose her words carefully. "You could spend the nights here until they transfer your bed. After all, it is *your* bed. And you'd have the bathroom and all, since no one else uses it."

Duke didn't want to agree too quickly. Keeping his smile from showing right away, he pretended to think it over. "It wouldn't bother you to have a strange man in your home?"

"I had one for years, and didn't seem to mind too much," she stated, tongue in cheek. At his laugh, she continued. "Why? Are you a serial killer in disguise?"

"No."

"A rapist?"

"No."

"Then I don't see what the problem is," she stated matter-of-factly. "I have your bedroom set and you have a choice between your floor, a hotel or your own bed for a good night's sleep."

He tried to look somber. "It's a true fact."

"Then pick your poison. After all, you can always stay at your place until you're ready for bed."

"That's a very generous offer. I appreciate the sacrifice. No matter how gracious you are, I know it's not easy sharing a space that's always been private before."

"It's not forever." She laughed just a little nervously. "Just a night or two until you can get your bed back."

"Well, then, before you change your mind, I accept."

Beth stood, a smile blooming. The beauty of it knocked the air from his lungs. He took a deep breath, forcing air back where it belonged.

"Before you change your mind, Mr. McGregor, and choose to sacrifice yourself to the floor gods, I'll make the bed."

Duke stood, too. "I can do that."

"Not this time. They're my sheets, so I'll do it. Sit and relax," she ordered. "Finish drinking your coffee and enjoy a few quiet moments. It will do you good."

She was gone instantly. Duke did as he was told because it suited him to do so.

He leaned back and enjoyed the sound of domesticity without the strings of old emotions tied to it. It sounded nice.

He had plenty of women who wanted to pamper him and demonstrate just how good they were at making him happy. But they had ulterior motives for doing so. They all wanted either marriage or support or both. Sex in exchange for security. He'd seen enough of that in the past two years. Now he dated many, so no one could hem him in.

But this woman had made him dinner and fresh coffee, then graciously offered him the use of her home—all in the name of friendship.

Right now, he liked Beth's mothering tendencies. But when he tired of that, he would tell her so. He'd never had a problem voicing his opinion.

In the meantime, her help was definitely being given in friendship, with no strings attached. She had no designs on him. She wasn't going to seduce him in the middle of the night. He could relax his guard....

Beth's voice interrupted his reverie. "Do you use a blanket?"

"What temperature do you keep the place at night?"

"Around sixty-eight."

"Just in case, yes, please."

"Good. Your bed is ready when you are."

Perfect timing. He took the last sip of his coffee and set the cup down.

"And the cup gets rinsed and put in the kitchen sink," she reminded gently.

"Of course." Damn! She even sounded like a mother! He did as he was told. "I'll be back in a little while," he said, heading for the door. "I need to make a few phone calls and get my stuff together."

She smiled brightly; this time it seemed fake to him and he wanted the real thing back. He wanted her full attention instead of the polite, mannerly attitude she was showing.

"I'll be up for the next half hour," she said, her hand on the doorknob. "I'm afraid tonight's an early night for me. Tomorrow's a rough day."

He grinned. "Don't worry. I won't be long. Half an hour at the latest." Duke stepped into the hallway and the door closed softly but securely behind him.

He walked down the hall taking deep breaths and telling himself to relax and place himself elsewhere. She was sexy as hell and not for him. Not for him at all . . .

Listening to his messages helped cool him down a little. Two were from female acquaintances, who were asking for an escort to this and that, one from a business associate, one regarding a charity he occasionally supported, and one hang-up. Nothing that couldn't wait.

He dumped a few toiletries into his leather shaving kit and grabbed the T-shirt and shorts he wore jogging, which would do just fine for tomorrow morning.

Just as Duke was ready to walk out the door, the phone rang. He debated letting the machine answer it, then decided against it. Only family would be calling this late in the evening.

He was right. It was Benjamin McGregor III. "Hey, Dad, how's it goin' down?"

"Everything's fine here. How's school? More important, how are your grades?"

"Nothing like putting a stop to the chitchat," his son replied ruefully.

Duke wasn't really worried about his son's grades. He was a math major at Texas A&M University and planned to be a statistician. Although Duke didn't know much about that particular field, he knew his son was more grown-up than most boys his age and had been working toward this career for years, taking every math course offered. The frosting on the cake, though, was that his son was also a sociable athlete. He was on the golf team and played polo on occasion. Not the chosen sports of the average nineteen-year-old, but certainly respectable. Duke was proud.

"Are you having a problem?"

"Naw, just trying to concentrate on the subject instead of all those *fine* females dancing around here."

"Speaking of fine females," Duke said slowly, his attention still on his hostess. "Do you remember the McGruder girls?"

"The twins?" Ben asked in a voice laced with surprise.

"The very ones."

"Sure, I do. They're going to University of Texas, but I don't know what they're majoring in."

"Did you know them?" Duke pressed.

"Of course I did, for most of my life. We went to the same elementary, middle and high school." He sounded offended. "They weren't that strong in math and sciences, but one was the lead in a couple of school plays and president of the drama club. The other one was a cheerleader."

"What did you think of them?"

"They're beautiful. Fine— Uh, really nice looking." His son hesitated on the description as if he could offend his father.

Duke grinned. Boys didn't change. He would have worried about his aged parents' reactions to describing a teenage girl, too.

"And what about their parents?"

"Their mother was so strict, most of the guys were afraid of her."

"Really?"

"Yeah." Ben was obviously warming to his subject. "I remember one of the guys saying Mrs. McGruder was such a dragon she could take on Saint George and win."

"I was just wondering," Duke said. His son's impression of Beth McGruder was not his, but kids always knew more about the neighbors than the adults did.

"Why? What's going down?"

"I bought a bed and it was accidentally delivered to Mrs. McGruder's condo, directly below me."

"Wow! Stay away from her, Dad. If you and Mom couldn't get along, you'd *really* have trouble with that woman."

"Ben," Duke began, ready to warn him to stay out of his parents' problems. Ben fluctuated between his mom and dad, and found it hard not to gripe to one about the other, even though he loved them both. Duke didn't want to hear it. It wouldn't do anyone any good to sympathize with his problems with the other parent. If he did, Ben would never come to terms with the divorce and the new role he needed to establish between himself and his parents.

"Okay, okay," Ben soothed. "Just a friendly word of warning, Dad. You don't need to get involved. You've got the perfect bachelor life."

"Gotcha, son. Thanks for the advice."

"No problem, Dad. By the way, you don't have an extra hundred, do you? My cycle needs a transmission tune-up."

Duke sighed. He hated that cycle but he was always forced into perpetuating its life. "How can a math major always come up shy on his budget?"

"It's hard work, but somebody's got to prove mathematicians are human and make mistakes like everyone else."

"It's in the mail. But that's it, Ben. If that damn thing dies after this, I'll say good riddance and have it hauled off to the junkyard."

"I hear you, Dad. Honest. Thanks a bunch, and I'll be talkin' to you later."

"Love you, son."

"Love you, Dad."

The phone went silent.

Suddenly Duke was exhausted. He picked up his clothing and walked out the door, making sure it was locked behind him. It was too late to go to a motel. He was too tired to sleep on the floor. He would have to brave Beth McGruder and worry about tomorrow night tomorrow.

He had distanced himself mentally from the woman by the time he reached her apartment.

Then she opened the door, and her smile was sweet, her bathrobe pink and fluffy and . . . she looked sexy.

It wasn't as if he didn't get out enough—he dated steadily. So why was he so . . . affected?

"There are sample-size shampoos and soaps in a basket in the linen closet there," she said, pointing to the guest bath. "And extra towels and washcloths. If you need anything else, please feel free to ask."

"Thanks," he replied, dropping his stuff on the newly made bed.

Beth hesitated in the doorway. "Coffeepot comes on at six in the morning. Help yourself to cream, and sugar's in the cabinet."

"Thanks," he repeated, leaning against the footboard and watching her. She didn't look like a dragon at all....

"Well, good night." She gave a lightning-quick smile and pulled back from the doorway.

"Good night."

Beth closed the door behind her very softly. Duke barely heard the click of the lock.

He continued to lean against the footboard of the bed, staring at the place where she'd stood just a moment earlier.

It crossed his mind to wonder why she hadn't been more flirtatious . . . more open . . . more sexual. Most women were, these days. He fleetingly wondered why she wasn't attracted to him, but refused to believe that there was something wrong with him. If only monetarily speaking, he was one hell of a catch. It had to be that "dragon" syndrome that kept her from getting too close to him.

To hell with that train of thought.

Ten minutes later he slipped between the cool sheets and gave a heavy sigh of exhaustion. The lights were off and the built-in stereo speakers were softly playing a slow country song.

But he couldn't sleep.

His imagination was playing tricks on him, carrying him into the other room, into that other fantasy bed, where a golden-haired woman beckoned him with her sexy ways and sweet strokes. He imagined her seducing him into an unbelievable pleasure, and the image was so powerful he didn't dare drift off, in case he walked in his sleep.

3

AFTER BRUSHING HER teeth, Beth climbed up into her bed and stared around the room. Duke was right; it was certainly her fantasy bed—perhaps her only realizable fantasy. And leave it to the man in the next room to point out just what was missing—as if she didn't already know.

A man she could share her fantasy with—a man like Duke—would have made the fantasy complete.

A man who would take her in his arms and make her feel she'd just reached shelter. And bliss. And romance. And . . .

Warning bells rang in her head. *Wrong!* The word sang through her body. What was she thinking of? She didn't need a man to screw up her emotions now that she'd just found a healthy balance again. Wasn't one bad relationship enough for a lifetime? Of course it was. But there was a tinge of doubt in her mind's voice.

She lifted her head and tilted her chin determinedly. This bed was exactly what she wanted: a fantasy. She could imagine Duke being in this bed all night long and it would never hurt either of them. As long as it wasn't real, it wouldn't even be wrong. She fell asleep, content in the knowledge that she could still be in control of her own fragile emotions. All she needed was a little nerve to say no to any fantasy that didn't feel right.

But the next morning Beth woke feeling as if she'd tossed and turned all night without a wink of sleep. She had done just what she'd said she would; she'd kept her fantasy bed and her fantasy man busy all night. They'd conversed with a mattress width between them, arguing about making love. And no one knew about their liaison but Beth herself.

The morning brought reality. She paced the floor for over half an hour before she got up the nerve to knock on Duke's door and let him know there was fresh coffee outside his room.

She'd gotten up over an hour before the alarm clock had dictated. Her dreams last night had been laced with sensuous pictures of the man in the other room: dressed and undressed, laughing and serious. But even in sleep she knew it was just a dream, not cold reality, because he never looked bad, and he never lost his temper. The word *temper* brought a shiver. She ignored it. She no longer had to deal with that worry— would never have to deal with *it* again.

Although her utter lack of sleep last night was unusual, she never had needed quite as much sleep as the average person. It was her habit to do all those tasks in the early morning that her friends saved for the evening. She ran the dishwasher, cleaned her bathroom and rode her stationary bike.

Her hand hovered hesitantly for a moment before she knocked briskly on the spare bedroom door. "Duke, it's time to wake up. There's coffee on the table just outside your door."

She heard a grunt, a groan and what sounded like a bear moving in his den. She smiled, then walked into her own bedroom, undid her robe and stepped into the shower. As far as she was concerned, her duty as a hostess was done.

DUKE HEARD THE SWEET tones of an angel, then realized it wasn't an angel, it was a siren—the very one from his earlier dreams. He sat bolt upright in bed and looked around. Not his bedroom, not his bed— Wait a minute, his foggy brain told him. This *was* his bed, he just hadn't slept in it until now. But this *wasn't* his bedroom; it belonged to the woman who'd been invading his dreams all night long.

He stood and stretched, then picked up his running shorts from the floor and slipped into them, sans underwear. He could hear the shower going in the other bathroom. He felt pretty safe.

Opening the door, he poked his head out and found the coast clear. It was with a little disappointment at not seeing Beth that Duke reached for the fresh cup of coffee sitting on the table by his door. It was hot and black. Just the way he liked it.

Then he did what he usually did in the morning; he took his coffee cup through the French doors leading to the patio and stared at the sunrise. At home, this was where he came to gather his thoughts and get a handle on the day's activities.

One of the things he had liked about his condo when he rented it was the view. Since the bowed patio faced south, he could see both sunrise and sunset. Beth had the exact view he had, except she was one floor closer to the ground.

He took a deep breath of early-morning air and marveled at the clean snap of it. He counted himself lucky to live outside Houston, among the trees, although the gas and time it took to go back and forth to work or parties or plays, or anything else that a busy social life demanded, was a definite minus.

He'd been waiting for Ben to enter college before doing something so drastic as moving away from the neighborhood his son knew as home. He had promised to keep the homestead payments going until Benjamin had been in school for one semester, and everyone had adjusted to a new way of life. By the end of this year, his wife—ex-wife—would assume full responsibility for the house. Then he would move to a location better suited to a bachelor businessman— closer to town, perhaps in the Galleria area....

He heard a faint rustling behind him and turned.

Beth looked all clean and scrubbed, like a little girl. A *sexy* little girl. She was in that same fluffy pink robe she'd worn last night, only was now sporting a matching towel wrapped around her head, turban-style. Her skin glowed and she wore a smile that made the sunshine seem brighter.

"Good morning," she said, a happy lilt in her voice.

"Good morning." He sounded far gruffer than he felt. He cleared his voice and tried to do the same with his thoughts. Instead, his mind played tricks on him, dissolving the pink bathrobe.... "I was just enjoying the sunrise," he managed to say.

Her eyes crinkled in laughter. "You were asleep during the sunrise over forty-five minutes ago. This is just early morning."

"I'm glad you're here to share that with me. I might never have known." His own grin took the sting away from his words and added the teasing note she responded to so well.

She was quick with an answer. "It's my job to keep the world on an even keel and make sure that no one passes on erroneous information."

"That's quite a job description. What's your title?"

"Queen Beth," she replied, deadpan.

"I'm glad I asked," he muttered as he took a gulp of his coffee. "I might not have bowed in time."

"Then you'd *really* be in trouble, Sir Knight. No one would let you sit at the table."

"Table?"

"The Round Table."

He laughed another belly laugh, the second in two days. That was unusual.

"What time do you have to be at work?" she asked.

"I'm going directly to an appointment around ten-thirty. I'll check with the office just before I leave."

Beth took a step back, and he realized he wanted to hold her there on the patio with him for a little while longer. He wanted her to enjoy the beginning of a beautiful day—a day he probably wouldn't have given more than a cursory glance if she hadn't been here to share it with him.

"I've got to get dressed. May I join you for another cup of coffee in a few minutes?"

"Be my guest," he replied, sitting in the lawn chair. He leaned back as if he had all the time in the world, and suddenly he felt as if he really did. He heard his favorite newscaster's voice coming from the living room TV and realized she was watching the same program he usually tuned in to before work.

Great. He had coffee, a sunrise—correction, an early-morning sun bask—and the news. *And* he couldn't hear his own phone ringing to tell him of a thousand different problems that needed to be solved right away.

His son's words of warning came back to him, but he shoved aside visions of a dragon lady. After all, he was only playing hooky in the woman's apartment, not committing himself to a lifetime of . . .

Duke leaned his head back and closed his eyes, giving a sigh that pronounced his entire body relaxed. Within seconds, his eyes drifted shut and he reveled in the heat of the sun and the comforting sound of the birds playing hide-and-seek among the boughs of the tall pine.

He smelled her perfume first. It wrapped around him like a sensuous blanket. When he opened his eyes she was replacing the mug at his side with a fresh cup of coffee. He sat up straight, saying, "Thanks. I didn't mean for you to wait on me."

"I know. But I was getting one for myself, so it was no bother."

She was dressed in a maroon power suit with a deeper-colored camisole underneath. The hem of the skirt was several inches above her knees, showing off a pair of shapely legs. He glanced down and saw that she wore high heels, which made those legs look even longer.

Sexy. Very sexy.

"Mind if I sit down?" she asked, still standing, holding her coffee.

"Of course not." Acting casual, he leaned back again and watched her slip into the chair next to him. She was so graceful.

"Hmm," she said, staring out at the treetops just as he'd done when he first stepped outside. "I love this time of morning. It's always been my favorite part of the day."

"Mine, too," Duke half lied. *It used to be*, he added silently in his own defense. These days, he was either in his car on the way to some appointment or already at the office by this hour. "Do you usually go to work this late?"

Beth did what Duke had done earlier. She directed her face toward the rays of the sun, closed her eyes and smiled. "I have to be there by eight-thirty."

"When do you come home?"

"Around six." She squinted one eye and looked over at him. "Once I'm home, you're welcome to come down any time."

"Thanks," he said shortly. "But I have a dinner date that will last until ten-thirty or so."

She'd closed her eyes again, and she looked so serene. Obviously his mention of a dinner date hadn't bothered her. "No problem. As long as it's not after eleven-thirty. After that, you can count on using your floor or a friend's place. Or that hotel you were thinking about."

He felt a momentary rush of irritation, but quelled it. She didn't have to care so little. "Thanks. I'll be sure to make my curfew. By the way, I'd still like to pay you for your trouble."

"No need. It's your bed and you're entitled to it. After all, it wasn't your mistake."

Did she have to be so damn practical? Couldn't she *gush* a little at his generosity? "I insist."

"We'll discuss it later," she countered.

Miffed that she wasn't appreciative of his offer, he decided that maybe Ben was right about Beth McGruder's personality.

Duke stood and stretched, then turned toward the door. "See you later."

Beth looked at her watch, then got up and followed him. "Have a good day," she called, walking toward her own room. Two minutes later Duke had grabbed his shaving kit and suit from the spare room and was heading for the door. Beth came from her room at the same moment and they left the apartment together. Duke stood by while she locked the door behind them.

Just then, Mrs. Rutgar cracked her door and peered through the chained opening. "Is everything all right?"

For the first time since he'd met her, Beth looked flustered. He gave the nosy neighbor his most engaging smile. "Good morning, Mrs. Rutgar," he said. "Everything's fine. It's a beautiful day, isn't it?"

One eye narrowed on him, then darted down to the suit over his arm and the loop of the leather kit bag hanging from his finger.

It was too much to resist. "Of course, this morning could be special because I haven't had such a good night's sleep in a long time." He turned to Beth. "Thanks again." Then his voice dropped to a low, sexy tone that held unspoken promises of long, wonderful hours of lovemaking. "I'll see you tonight, before eleven."

Beth's face had turned red enough to match her suit, before he turned and strolled down the hallway toward the elevators. He was whistling a snappy little tune as the doors slid shut behind him.

He hadn't felt so lighthearted in years.

BETH FELT HER ENTIRE body blushing. Damn that man!

She tried to think of something clever or witty to say to her neighbor, but she couldn't. Instead, she looked at Mrs. Rutgar's partially open door, smiled and shrugged. "Have a good day." It was all she could think of to say.

Walking down the hallway toward the indented bank of elevators, she hoped and prayed that she wouldn't run into Duke McGregor. Not while she was still recovering from his sexy "act." She felt like a fool, and she needed time alone to think.

All night long she'd tossed and turned, nervous, but also happy in the knowledge that there was a man— a protector—in the house. When she awoke, she was frustrated with herself for even having the feeling.

Then she hadn't wanted the morning to end; had even taken a little extra time to spend with him out on the patio. She didn't like that. It wasn't fair that he should push all her old buttons and make her feel so— so—feminine! She didn't want to fall into the trap of getting all mushy and soft and nurturing with a man. It didn't work for her. Men usually took her brand of caring to be mothering. *Mothering!* Didn't men realize the difference between mothering and caring? Were they nuts? Was Duke McGregor the same way? She would bet he was.

And then he'd had the nerve to insult her by implying to a nosy neighbor that they were having an affair! Didn't he see how that cheapened her? His idea of a joke was her idea of personal embarrassment!

She pulled out of the underground garage and slipped into traffic, heading toward the office. Her mind whirled with questions and answers that didn't necessarily match up.

Duke had said he wasn't going to be home until late.

Fine. She wouldn't think about his "dinner date," although curiosity was killing her. Curiosity and something else... Jealousy? It couldn't be. She totally denied that emotion.

She was going out herself, tonight, with three other women, just as she had planned. It would be a fun evening, full of laughter and tears as they brought each other up to date on their lives. And if it wasn't fun, she would pretend it was, darn it!

That thought took away a little of the frustration she felt.

All day long at work she was consumed by thoughts of the man who had unexpectedly entered her life and left such a lasting impression. Normally, she was good at her job because she was detail oriented, but today she'd pulled one wrong file, then had made two mistakes on letters and hadn't caught them before her boss saw the errors.

But one good thing did come of it. By noon she was certain she'd imagined most of Duke's sex appeal and had decided that her attraction to him was simply the result of not having had a man in her life for a long time.

As she moved through the day, Beth was forever grateful to be working with her friend Mary, who had helped her find this secretarial job. Over lunch, they talked about everything—everything except Duke's instant appearance into her life. That was a topic Beth wasn't prepared to discuss right now. But her new bed was another matter, and she told Mary all about it.

At five o'clock, she and Mary left the office together and drove to the restaurant the friends had chosen for their weekly get-together. Tonight, they were eating Mexican. By the time she'd had a margarita or two, some spicy hot nachos, and lots of great conversation and laughter, she was convinced her earlier attitude was only a momentary lapse of sanity. She didn't want, wasn't ready for, any man, let alone the one who had spent the night in her condo.

She was quite happy socializing with her friends. The six women had met while working for the same temporary service agency several years ago. They'd ended up temping for a large insurance company where the rest of the employees didn't consider them to be permanent or important, so their relationships had cemented over lunches together, when they began to tell each other the ups and downs of their lives, as strangers do often enough. It was Beth's first job outside the home, but at the time, her daughters had been in high school and she'd thought it might be wise to sharpen her secretarial skills and find a new challenge. Her job as a mother was almost over.

The temporary positions had ended, but the friendships had not. Ever since the insurance company days, the six women had met once a week ex-

cept at Christmas. They officially called themselves
the Tuesday Nite Bunco group without Bunco. Maureen had said she thought they should call it the
Chicken Soup Group, since she always felt as if her
soul had been nourished after their evenings of sharing. Maureen, Mary, Kay and Linda were certainly
Beth's good friends. Their bonding meant that each
of them had someone to gripe to who understood.
Sometimes it just involved spending a couple of hours
having fun and easy conversation before they all went
their own ways.

Mary and Beth were the last to arrive.

Kay was in the middle of a thought-provoking
statement. "So I decided, all I want is someone gentle, loving and caring. Is that too much to ask from a
millionaire?"

The waitress came by just as Beth slipped into her
chair and slid out of her heels. She joined in the
laughter. "Good point, Kay. Except, where in the
world are you going to meet a millionaire? And what
would you do with him once you found him?"

"He's going to walk into my life one day and I'll be
ready for him. I'll be sweet and kind and loving and
give him whatever he wants. He won't have a chance
to think of life without me. Then, I'll eat a banana and
leave the peel on the floor just as he finishes his 'I
do's.'"

"There's a charming thought," Mary drawled. "At
that rate he won't even have time to write a will. Why
would you marry a guy you don't want to be with?

You'd only have to find someone else to spend the rest of your life with. Why not someone you love? Besides, you just graduated from nursing school, you've got a new career you love and a house that anyone could feel cozy in."

Kay snorted. "I agree. We're smart, funny and fun. We ought to just go through life as if there were no men out there, waiting for the opportunity of a lifetime. Which is us, of course. There's someone out there waiting for me to enter his dreary life and make it sparkle with love and laughter and anticipation of everything there is to come. Then again, he might not show up until I'm old and gray. By then, I won't care."

"By then, neither will he," Linda countered, her blond curls bobbing in emphasis. "But the sad thing is, you might never have babies together."

"Great." Mary sounded disgusted with herself. "He wants babies and I just had my tubes tied. I thought I had it made, and now I find I can't give him what would make him happy. All the joy in my life is gone."

"Good grief, Mary," Beth exclaimed, usually the logical one when it came to fantasies—except for her bed, of course. "There *isn't* a he or him in your life!"

"I know," she answered calmly before biting into a jalapeño-laden chip. "But if there was, he'd be *so* disappointed when I told him we'd be childless."

Once more, the women laughed at their friend's brittle humor.

When the waitress brought their frozen drinks, Beth raised her glass in a toast. "Here's to more laughter in our lives. And may the best woman win in the battle of the sexes."

"Here, here!"

"Right on, right on!"

"And may the battle end soon so we can all get on with living and loving with those wonderful, sensitive, housebroken partners."

Then they sipped at the frosty drinks.

"I've got a date tomorrow night," Maureen announced. "I think it's my first in over three months."

Everyone was full of questions, but Beth's won out. "Where did you meet him?"

"He came into the hotel and asked for a king-size smoking room. I explained to him that we didn't have one available and he was crushed." Maureen worked at the front desk of a hotel that relied on airport business. It was constantly busy with single-night guests who were on their way to or from somewhere, and never really wanted more from a woman than an uninvolved one-night stand. Maureen was rightfully wary of the hotel's guests.

"You're dating a *smoker*? I thought little Sam was allergic to smoke," Kay said, referring to her friend's youngest son, a nine-year-old who was ill more often than he wasn't. "Doesn't he always have bronchitis?"

"That's why he wanted the room," Maureen explained. "He gave it up two weeks ago, but he still likes to catch a whiff of smoke occasionally. It keeps him from feeling deprived."

"Great," Beth declared. "Instead, he gets second-hand smoke, which is supposed to be worse for you than firsthand. Although I never did understand that."

"At least he's trying," Maureen defended. "Besides. I used to smoke, too. I understand how he feels."

"Okay, I remember," Beth said in a placating tone. "I'm not always so quick to tear dreams apart, but I remember how hard it was for you to quit."

Maureen gave her a grin and continued talking about her new date.

Beth sipped on her drink and listened to her friends banter back and forth. She had to smile at them—and laugh a little at her own used-to-be self. Years ago, any banter or debate would have frightened her, and she would have left the scene. Her father had been an angry man. She recalled how his debates had always ended in arguments, and her memories of his rage weren't far behind. Because of that, she'd never learned how to deal with anger. Or at least, not until her father had died. Now, however, she'd grown up and could "discuss" with the best—as long as strong emotions weren't involved.

With this group she felt safe and could voice thoughts and opinions she might not have brought up with others she didn't trust as well. Through these weekly get-togethers, though, they had built a mutual trust that beat anything else she'd ever known.

Two of them were married, two were divorced and one of them had never married, but was in a relationship that had lasted five years. All of them agreed that this kind of evening made them appreciate what they had. Linda and Wanda, for example, said they went home and kissed their mates in deep gratitude for sticking around.

"Are you excited, Maureen? Is he nice?" asked Kay in a soft voice, leaning forward. Kay was so shy that they all babied her, in case she darted away emotionally like a sprite.

Maureen grinned. "He's so very nice. And he's just a little shy. He's been divorced for over a year, and since then he hasn't had a relationship with anyone."

"How long have you two known each other?" Beth asked.

"Off and on, he's been a guest in the hotel for about six months."

"And he's just now getting around to asking you out? No wonder he hasn't been in a relationship!" Mary snorted. "At the rate he's going, you won't have a second date until next year."

"Don't pay any attention to her," Linda soothed. "She's just jealous that she hasn't had a date this year. It's already October and by this time, she ought to be trying to squirm out of an affair that went wrong."

"Not me," Kay stated. "I've got a guy that's worth his weight in salt. As a matter of fact, he's wallpapering tonight, as we speak." She gave an exaggerated sigh. "What a great guy."

And he was. It was nice to know that Kay appreciated the man who seemed to love her to distraction. She would do anything for him except marry him.

"Bitch." Mary grinned. "The only reason we keep you in this bunco group is because you and your two cohorts remind us that there is a chance for happiness in a world gone crazy around divorce. And this guy might not be Mr. Right, but he's right for now."

"Yes, by all means, enjoy him," Beth interjected as she tilted her drink toward her friend in a salute. "Mary's right. She and I have nothing better to do than worry about other people's lives. Goodness knows, none of us seems to have a man of our own to mess up our own lives."

"Beth? What's going on in your life?" Kay asked, turning her attention from one friend to another.

"After your last statement, I guess nothing." Beth laughed.

"Did they ever deliver your fantasy bed?"

"Yesterday," she confirmed. "And it's wonderful. Exactly what I wanted."

"Do those fabulous bed linens we found at Macy's look as wonderful as you thought they would?"

Beth remembered how the white comforter and overstuffed, goose-down pillows had looked this morning when she made up the bed. "Better. I'll have you all over for dinner and show it off. It looks like something out of *The Thousand and One Nights*."

"When is this dinner?" Linda asked, reaching for another chip and dipping it into the salsa.

An image of Duke sitting on the balcony in nothing but a pair of wrinkled shorts flashed through her mind and she felt her face flush. "Soon. Sometime in the next three weeks."

It was good to be with friends, but she wasn't brave enough to bring Duke into the conversation right now. Perhaps later, when he was sleeping in his own apartment and her life had returned to its usual, steady pace. Then she would make up a funny story about the whole weird episode and they would all have a good laugh.

That thought settled her nerves. Soon, everything would return to normal and she would be secure again, instead of wondering what it would be like to kiss a man she hardly knew.

The conversation turned to work and Beth felt her tension ease further. By the time they ordered dinner, she was completely relaxed. It paid to see friends and get her mind off "other" things.

By nine-thirty the rest of the women were ready to wind up the evening. Beth stood and gave them each a hug as they filed out of the booth and into the muggy night air. A light, cool breeze had sprung up and it felt heavenly, blowing through her hair.

"Beth?" Kay touched her on the shoulder. "You've been so quiet tonight. Is everything all right?"

She laughed. "Everything's fine. I'm just glad to sit back and listen to you all gripe for a change."

"How's work?"

"Work's fine, but it's been a long day. I'm worn-out," Beth lied. She took out her keys from her purse. "Don't worry. I'll call you later in the week."

"Well, if you're sure..." Kay said, then added, "Maybe we can take in a movie Friday night. My better half will be out to a sports-car show for the evening."

"Sure," Beth answered. "Yes."

After one last hug, Kay ran to her car holding her hair in place. Beth, on the other hand, walked, reveling in the breeze against her skin.

She drove home with the windows down and kept staring up at the star-studded sky. It was peaceful and calm, and although she was physically tired, she was at peace with the world. It was a nice feeling—one that came more often now that the crazy time of her divorce and all the uncertainty had ended and her life had become a dependable routine. Nice and quiet and predictable.

"And what's wrong with 'predictable'?" she asked the dark, night sky.

There was no answer.

But she knew what was wrong. The predictable life was one that was lived alone. Mix in just one other person and you created a completely different recipe.

Mix in a person like Duke McGregor, and . . .

Her blood flowed faster through her veins at the thought of going home and seeing him there tonight.

Pulling into the underground garage, she told herself it was okay to look forward to seeing Duke. It was natural. It was— She braked for the cherry red BMW parked in front of the elevators, blocking her way.

Her attention was instantly drawn to the two people who were using the driver's-side door as a leaning post. They were wrapped in each other's arms, lips searching lips. The woman was a tall sun-kissed blonde and she was leaning back against the car as if she were warm wax. She held the man's head between long, crimson-tipped fingers.

The man was Duke McGregor. And he was no innocent bystander. His arms were bracketing her body, his hands resting on the roof of the car as he leaned toward her. His well-muscled torso seemed to be touching every part of hers.

Beth waited for a moment, then decided it looked like an all-night thing. She tooted her horn. Duke pulled back and looked over at her, but the woman took her time. Finally, she pulled away and glanced at Beth, irritation marring her aristocratic brow.

Beth felt a bunch satisfied to be breaking up the tête-à-tête. Unrepentant, she waved her fingers and smiled innocently.

Duke had recognized her instantly, and his deepening frown was her reward. At least she'd found a little pleasure in his obvious discomfort.

He turned back to the woman in his arms and gave her a big smile just before placing a soft kiss on her forehead. After murmuring a few words, he opened the BMW's driver-side door and settled her into the plush leather seat. Another thirty seconds and the BMW was wheeling down the aisle and out the exit.

Beth carefully pulled into her space. She was even more careful as she locked the doors and secured the car, keeping her eyes focused on that instead of on Duke.

When she reached the elevator, he was waiting for her, his frown still in place.

They stepped into the cubicle and both turned to face the front.

Beth finally spoke as the doors closed. "Sorry about the interruption."

"No need to be. We were blocking the way."

"I know, but . . ." She didn't know what to say. *I know, but the ache in the pit of my stomach makes me want to kick your shins so you'll feel as bad as I do.* It didn't make any sense. She hardly knew the man, yet she was feeling betrayed. As if they'd been together for years!

"Judy is a woman I date occasionally." His voice was low, his gaze completely focused on the elevator window announcing each floor.

"She's beautiful."

"We were breaking up this evening."

"Funny, I've never seen anyone break up by making kissyface in a dim underground parking area," Beth said in mock innocence.

Duke sighed in resignation. "I know. I just don't want to hurt her feelings. She's a good friend."

A likely story. "I see."

She did see—that he wanted her to believe there was nothing to it. And in spite of it all, she wanted to believe the same thing. It made her feel better. When the elevator finally came to her floor, the doors opened. "See you," she said.

As the doors were closing, Duke punched the Hold button and leaned out. "Am I still welcome?"

Her eyebrows rose, along with her spirits. "Of course."

His smile was quick to come, and quick to go. "I'll be there in half an hour."

"See you then." She continued down the hall, and there was still a smile on her face when she opened the door to her condo.

She heard the door across the hall creak.

Instead of being bothered, Beth waved across the corridor and said, "Good evening Mrs. Rutgar. Beautiful evening, isn't it?"

"Beautiful evening," the widow repeated, with an odd lilt in her voice. The chain rattled as the door closed.

Beth sighed. Maybe she didn't have a man in her life, but at least she wasn't afraid to open her door and let life in.

The question was, Did she have the courage to open her door and let *Duke* in?

4

As far as Duke was concerned, Judy was no longer a romantic interest in his life. He had made the right decision, breaking up with her; he knew that, because he felt a great load had been lifted from his shoulders after all was said and done and she'd finally driven away. Oh, he knew he hadn't broken it off completely yet, but the first steps had been taken. He'd done everything but tell her he didn't want to see her again. His words and actions underlined that he was not the let's-settle-down-and-make-a-go-of-this-relationship kind of guy. She even knew he was dating other women—other women who also dated other men and certainly didn't make a commitment out of him.

And then there was Beth.

He was amazed that she'd never said another word about that night in the garage. Most women would have questioned him raw. There were no tears and recriminations from Beth. She accepted him at his word. It was one of the best feelings in the world to know that someone believed you—that someone knew you were as good as your word.

Not that this had anything to do with Beth. After all, she wasn't taking Judy's place. Beth was only a friend. . . .

Bull, buddy boy, his conscience stated unequivocally. But he ignored that. He certainly wasn't ready to commit to anyone, and he doubted if Beth was ready to do that, either. They didn't need to hop into bed together to recognize where this was eventually heading. Maybe. Maybe they would never make it into a deep relationship. But they would always be friends.

That load of hogwash made him feel more comfortable, so he believed it.

His business was hectic. Quarterly corporate taxes had to be filed and the entire office was humming with overwork. Once this week was done, things would die down a little and they would all have an extra day off during the week. But right now the push was on to complete and electronically mail all the paperwork that would hopefully keep his clients and the IRS happy.

Three days later, Duke's personal secretary, Susan, popped her head around the corner of his office door. "Duke?" Her usual bright smile was missing. Instead she wore a disgusted look. "I called the furniture company to see about moving your bed to your place. The girl who answered the phone was so confused it took over fifteen minutes to get an answer."

"They're going out of business," Duke guessed, but by the look on Susan's face, she already knew it was true.

"And no wonder. They're so disorganized, no one knows what's going on. I'm surprised they didn't close their doors a lot sooner than they did."

"Did they say when they could make the exchange?"

"They promised to get to you in about two weeks, when they've delivered everything else that's been sold." She tried to look sad. "Sorry, boss. You'll have to wait it out at your friendly neighbor's for a little while longer."

Duke tossed down his pen and leaned back in his leather chair. "You enjoy my discomfort, don't you?"

She grinned even wider. "You bet."

"Why? I write your paychecks on time. I don't yell—much. Why would you want to see me so uncomfortable?"

"Because your discomfort is nothing compared to your lady love's. She's angry as all get-out because you're not at your home where she can keep an eagle eye on you."

Susan was nothing if not honest. She didn't like Judy and the feeling was reciprocated. Duke tried to stay out of it. He needed his secretary; the other women in his life were only there to keep him from being bored and lonely. Although his relationship with Judy was almost over, he didn't want to tell Susan, knowing she would crow about it.

"You're heartless," he complained with a grin.

"And you love it. That same heartlessness keeps the rest of the wolves—business and otherwise—at bay."

"Okay, okay. Check on a hotel or renting a bed for me, will you?"

"Will do."

Duke got back to work, knowing his secretary would do her best to solve the problem. He also knew he wasn't half as eager to make other arrangements as he pretended to be. The thought of sharing a cup of green tea just before bedtime with Beth had once made him feel as if he was ready for a rocking chair—until he'd actually done it. Now he looked forward to that particular activity. He'd never had green tea before in his life until her. It was calming and extremely comforting. The laughter that came along with it was proving to be addictive. And playing with thoughts of her body in his embrace, her blond hair drifting against his arm, her smoky eyes gazing into his, were, he was discovering, the things sweet dreams were made of.

He checked over some reports, made two more business appointments and okayed several of his clients' requests. Later that afternoon, Susan came in and plopped into the chair across from his desk. From the looks of her, she'd had a rough day.

"You deserve a raise," he said.

She grinned, knowing she already earned far more than most administrative assistants. "I do, but I can't earn more than you. It wouldn't look good."

"Thanks." He tossed down his pen. "What's up?"

"I can't find a bed for you unless you want to rent it for a month. I found a foldaway, but I can't imagine you being comfortable on it."

"Rent the bed for a month and tell them I'll call when I'm through with it in a week or two."

"They can't do that. They need a week's notice to schedule pickup."

"Did you tell them they could make double their money by renting it again in the same month?"

Susan gave him a look that told him he'd underestimated her. Again. "Oh, I think I might have mentioned that little fact."

Duke sighed. He hated ineptness. Here was some young punk who'd been made manager of a furniture-rental place and he couldn't bend the rules, even when they were in his favor. "Then find a moving company to transfer the bed from Beth's to my place."

"Can I do that first thing tomorrow? I've still got a few things to wrap up today."

He smiled. That suited him. "If you must."

Her answering smile said that she saw right through him. "Thanks." She started to get up, then hesitated. "By the way, how's Benjamin doing?"

Duke knew she had a soft spot for Ben, who'd worked for the company as a gofer over a few summers. "He's doing fine. I'm taking off early next week to visit him and take in a football game."

"Tell him to get back here and go to work. He should be paying back his dad instead of spending money," Susan pronounced. "That way I'll have him around for a little while. I can whip him into shape."

"Since he's on scholarship, I haven't had to pay much. I just need to send him an extra hundred once a week." Duke couldn't help the pride in his voice when he mentioned his son's scholarship. "I promised to let him throw a bachelor party at my place after the tax rush is over."

"Are you brave or just plain stupid?"

"We both know what my ex-wife says."

"In that case, you're wonderfully brave and I think it's great. Every man ought to 'suffer the little children.' It's not just a woman's job anymore."

"Get off your soapbox, Susan. I've gone the extra mile, and you know it."

She cocked a knowing brow. "Which is the only reason I can kid you about it. You've been a better mom than some of the female moms I've known. And before you ask, yes, that's the highest compliment I can give."

"Thanks." He knew she meant it.

"Nothin' to it, the way you do it," she said, quoting a saying kids used, then she disappeared.

Duke left early. The car phone rang all the way home, but he refused to answer. After pulling into the underground parking garage, he turned off the car and the phone. By the time he got to his apartment, he was ready to talk to his son. Then he could turn it all off. He was tired; tired of being on call to anyone and everyone. He was just plain tired.

He called Benjamin and, although Ben was glad to hear from his dad, he was heading out the door to a meeting and the pizza parlor and didn't have time for a chat.

A restlessness filled Duke. He paced the length and breadth of the area he lived in, noticing which picture was crooked, which counter needed an extra swipe, which towel hadn't been hung straight.

"I need help," he muttered to himself in disgust. Then he grinned and picked up the phone. Beth answered on the second ring.

"Are you busy or do you have an hour to spare?" he asked, direct and to the point.

"I'm busy but I have an hour to spare."

"Good. Meet me on the roof in thirty minutes. We can watch the sunset together like good neighbors. I'll bring the wine and cheese."

"I've never been on the roof." She sounded doubtful. "Is it safe?"

"Of course it's safe. I'd never put you in jeopardy. Just go to the top floor, then take the stairs."

Duke hung up the phone, feeling a surge of excitement he hadn't felt in years. He gathered up a first load of things and headed upstairs. At the exit to the roof, he flipped off the hidden alarm switch he'd seen management use when his connection to the satellite dish had been checked. The night was as balmy and beautiful as he'd imagined. Up here, it was magical.

On the second try he brought up the wine and the food.

Then he waited impatiently.

Some twenty minutes later, Beth carefully stepped out the exit door onto the asphalt roof, looking as if she expected it to cave in at any moment. Obviously, she was not accustomed to playing on rooftops.

"I'm over here," he greeted softly. "Let your eyes adjust to the darkness."

She stood very still, looking into the night, toward his voice. The full moon shone on her face, exposing her doubts, her fears . . . her anticipation. The same anticipation he felt. Very slowly, with the sensual movements he was beginning to know so well, she started walking toward him.

Duke bent down and lit a votive candle in a silver-and-glass container so she could follow the point of light. When she reached his side, he held out a glass of ruby-red wine. "Happy evening," he said, and kissed the tip of her nose.

Her smile was tentative, her delight unabashed. "Merry night," she replied, tilting her glass in salute before sipping from it.

"How about sitting and enjoying the night sky?" Duke pointed to the two brown beanbag chairs squashed together in front of an open picnic basket.

"Thank you," she said primly, perching gingerly on the faux leather. Her eyes widened as she sank into the seat.

"Goose down mixed with the usual stuffing," he murmured.

Her hazel eyes widened in disbelief. "You do roof-top picnics often enough to have custom-made chairs?"

"These used to be in the game room of our house. My son and I used to sit in them and watch TV." He sank into the other leather-and-down recliner and took a deep breath. The fragrant night air mingled with Beth's perfume and created a heady sweetness. The scent was almost irresistible. Almost. Duke cleared his throat. "Don't you still have a few things lying around for your girls from the days when you were married?"

"Of course. But nothing as comfortable or well-made as these. This is pure decadence."

"That's what I said when I found Benjamin making out with his girlfriend on one of these," he said wryly.

"I hope the girl wasn't embarrassed to tears," Beth chastised.

He gave her a look of pure innocence. "I'm not heartless—just a father. I told them both to leave my sight and that the teenage Delilah should never darken my poor, naive son's door again."

"Spoken like a true father. Always blame someone else's kid." She began to laugh. "I'm sure that solved the problem."

Duke tilted his head until he was staring down into her wide eyes, thinking her laughter was damn near infectious. All sorts of things were running through his mind, but few had to do with being a parent except in the most basic, primal sense of the word. "You know what they say. Out of Dad's sight, out of mind."

"I'm learning a whole new philosophy, and I must admit, it's very different from my own point of view." Beth's voice was soft, tinged with low, sexy laughter. As the minutes ticked by, she became more relaxed than he'd ever seen her. The moon shone in her eyes and he couldn't stop staring at her. If he hadn't known better, he would have sworn she was casting a moon spell over him. "It gives me an idea of what it's like to be one of your corporate clients."

Duke forced himself to look away. He set his wineglass on the asphalt next to him. "It's my job to educate the client to the best of my ability. Are you capable of being taught?" He leaned forward until their mouths were only inches apart. His heartbeat thudded heavily in his chest, his pulse thrummed through his body, and he felt some primitive emotion he couldn't name.

"I'll be learning on the last day of my life," she murmured, her warm breath caressing his lips.

He couldn't have stopped his reaction any more than he could have stopped the moon from traveling the night sky. As if of their own volition, his lips feather-brushed the softness of hers. Once. Twice. Three times.

Her lips parted, showing the straight white line of her teeth. Her lashes drifted down to brush her cheek, then she looked back up at him with a hooded gaze.

"Do that again until you get it right," she finally whispered. "Please."

"Now who's the teacher?"

"I am. You are. We both are."

Honesty. He liked that. When his lips touched hers, he swore that stars exploded, lighting the heavens with glorious colors. His breath caught in his throat. He put his arms around her shoulders, pulling her toward him until her breasts were flattened against his chest. Still he couldn't let go. His mouth moved over hers, feeling the soft, pliant woman react to his touch by giving a gentle shiver. He felt her muscles relax, allowing her to glide against him. It was the sexiest move he'd ever felt.

Her arms encircling his neck, her fingers playing in his hair and sensuously stroking the back of his neck and shoulders, she leaned into him. Her tongue darted out and met his, then hid again, teasing him into playing hide-and-seek. Pleasure ran through his body like liquid mercury: strong, hot and lethal.

Duke cupped her face with his hands, holding her still while he searched her mouth to find every bit of softness there. She moaned and at the sound, his heart beat so heavily in his chest he thought it might break his ribs.

He wanted the kiss to go on and on, but when Beth pulled away, he sighed and let her loose. Her hands drifted lightly down his shoulders to his forearms and she tucked her head against his chest, keeping her face from him.

"Are you all right?" How could his voice sound so gruff when he felt so tender?

She nodded, sensuously rubbing her head against his chest. As if charged with electricity, strands of her golden hair clung to his shirt.

Feelings he'd thought were long dead in him came surging forward as he held her protectively against his chest. From where her hands touched his waist, warm sensations radiated to other parts of his body. "How am I doing on the learning scale?" he finally managed to utter.

"Einstein mentality. Richard Gere sex appeal."

"Wow," he said, his vision still slightly blurred by the brilliance of the stars in his head. "I must be better than I thought."

"Too much for this woman to handle," she answered in a shaky voice.

"I doubt that. After all, you were my inspiration."

"And you're truly Irish," she teased, finally pulling away from his chest and turning slightly to face the dark night sky. She was still cradled in his arms but now with her back to him and his arms around her waist. She gave a sigh and stared up at the night brilliance. "You've kissed the Blarney stone more than a few times."

He ran his thumb over one of her ribs in an almost-absentminded way. The scent of her hair was the same as her perfume, or maybe it was just the scent of a woman—this woman—that hung like a fragrant backdrop to the night.

He put the brakes on that train of thought. The last time he'd been drawn to a woman's scent was when he'd met his ex-wife. No one since, not even Judy, had aroused his senses that way. And now, here was Beth, her scent calling to his hormones in a way he'd thought he would never be called again.

At last, he remembered to speak. "Scottish. I'm Scottish."

"I thought so, but you know how borders are. My bet is that your people didn't care to have boundaries imposed on them and probably plundered their way through Ireland whenever they felt like it."

"Like barbarians?"

"Yes." She took a deep breath and let it out slowly. "Exactly."

He felt the rise and fall of her breathing beneath his fingers, and wanted to feel more. "Like the barbarians who slept in tents done up like your bedroom?"

He felt her back and shoulder muscles tighten, but she didn't move out of his arms. "Yes." It was only one word and she said it quietly, but it said so very much.

"Our fantasies aren't that different after all, Beth." He pulled her gently toward him until she was sitting in his lap, her body resting against his. Duke followed Beth's stare into the darkness surrounding them, enjoying the sounds of faraway civilization mixed with the occasional hoot of an owl and the sound of tree crickets seeking their mates. "The dark leather on my bed conjures up hunting pelts for warmth and comfort."

"And the overhead mirror?" Beth asked. "I'm sure that must have some primal meaning—besides appealing to narcissism or voyeurism, of course."

Duke thought quickly. "A reflection of the watering hole where man met beast and shared a moment of peace."

"Wow," she drawled. "You're good. You've very good. I underestimated you completely."

He chuckled in her ear, teasing it first with a light kiss. "No, you didn't."

She laughed, too. It was a dark, throaty sound that ran along his spine like a thousand sexy fingers. "You're right. I knew all along you were good. You just confirmed it."

Another long moment of silence stretched between them; Duke was amazed that he didn't feel uncomfortable. Normally he was impatient at this stage—he would either be ready to move on to the next stage by taking her to bed and making love to her, or he would be ready to leave her behind and be by himself.

Beth pointed up at the sky. "Look! A shooting star!"

"Make a wish," he ordered throatily. "But since I'm here, you have to include me in it."

She thought for a moment, then spoke slowly. "All right. I wish we both find the happiness we deserve."

"For tonight?"

"For always."

Reason took hold. This was sex calling to him, not a fairy-tale ending to some wonderful love story. He wouldn't get caught in that trap. Never again.

"Haven't you learned yet that there is no 'always,' Beth?"

"Sure, there is."

Her statement was so confident that suddenly, he wanted her to convince him of that. He wanted to believe.... "You were married for over twenty years. Wasn't that supposed to be for always?"

"Well, yes. But because my marriage didn't last forever doesn't mean there's no such thing as 'forever.'"

"Don't you think that's a little childish? Who do you know with an 'always' in their lives?"

"I grant you there aren't many. But that doesn't mean there are none. I have a few friends who still believe in 'always,' and they've been married long enough to prove it."

Duke bent forward and placed several butterfly kisses on her nape. She smelled so damn good, and she tilted her head to allow him easier access. "I'm glad you made the wish," he murmured between kisses. "Because just in case there is such a thing, I want to be on the receiving end."

"For always?"

"For now *and* for always."

Beth leaned forward, out of his reach, and retrieved her wineglass. She took a sip, then moved sideways so she could look up at him. "We're not making love, Duke."

He gave a lopsided grin. "Somehow I knew you'd say that. Did you think I was asking?"

"I don't know."

"I wouldn't push you into that. That's why I didn't ask."

"I'm sorry." She ducked her head so he couldn't see her expression, and sighed. "I just had a knee-jerk emotional reaction to your kiss."

He didn't want to admit that he felt exactly the same way. That kiss had left him wanting her in the worst way. "Meaning that you thought I needed more?"

"Meaning that I thought you *expected* more."

He swallowed the need in his throat. "It's okay." His hand soothed her ribs, stopping just below the fullness of her breast. He wanted to touch her nipple, feel the pebble hardness of it in his fingers, taste it with his tongue....

She gave a chuckle. "When I was a kid, my mom told me that guys think of sex every ten minutes."

He cleared his throat and found his voice. "Really? What did your dad tell you?"

"That she was wrong. It was every minute."

Duke sighed. "He was right."

"Even now?"

"Yes."

She looked over her shoulder, her eyes wide in the moonlight. "Still?"

"Still. At least, when I'm holding *you* in my arms," he admitted with more candor than he'd ever dared before. He slipped his hand under her blouse and felt the softness of her skin for the very first time. His pulse was throbbing so strongly, he thought the whole world must be able to hear the sound.

She looked away, back into the night; he felt her body tense. "Oh," she said.

"But as a male grows up, he learns there are other issues tied to the original impulse."

"Such as?"

"Such as romance and intimacy. Such as being intellectually compatible. Making love only takes an hour or so, but talking can be an all-day deal." He thought of Judy, and realized they never talked. "Such as needing more than sex from a relationship."

She snuggled back into his arms and onto his lap. "Oh."

Everything he said was the truth, so why did he feel like such a liar? It was because he didn't practice what he preached in his new dating life—at least, not until now. Not until Beth.

For the first time in a very long time he felt more than compatible with the woman in his arms. He *did* want more than sex—he wanted the romance, the excitement of anticipation instead of the immediate culmination. He wanted a relationship where he felt connected.

It dawned on him that this was a hell of a time to get a conscience. Whether he admitted it to himself or not, Duke had brought her up here with seduction in mind. He tried to tell himself that it was something to do to pass an evening when there was nothing else on the calendar.

Rotten reason.

Rotten excuse.

Beth drank the last drop of her wine. Instead of filling her glass again, Duke gave an exaggerated sigh.

"This was wonderful, but I'm afraid it's time to close the show and go to bed." He felt her tense again and realized his choice of words set off all kinds of alarms, especially in light of their conversation. He quickly attempted to relieve the stress. "This is quarterly tax time, and everyone thinks I need to take care of them first."

He didn't know if she bought his excuse, but Beth stood and brushed off her slacks as if she'd been sitting on sand. He watched where her hands were, then watched her hips sway with the motion.

She looked down at him and extended a hand. He reached out and as she pulled, he stood, amazed that such a tiny woman would have such strength.

Her gaze landed everywhere but on him. She looked around, picked up both glasses and began fussing with the picnic basket, loading the glasses along with the corked bottle of wine. In one smooth motion, she picked up the basket and one of the beanbag chairs. The only thing left was the other chair.

Duke looked at it, then at her. She was almost at the rooftop door. He swooped up the chair by its looped handle and took off after her. "Do you always carry and cart so well?" he asked, taking the basket from her hand. They continued to walk down the stairs to the elevator.

"I'm sorry. It's an old habit from when the kids were young. I usually had to carry almost everything. They would skip ahead and leave me holding the bag, so to speak."

He punched the elevator button. "Husband included?"

"Husband wasn't around most of the time."

"Where was 'husband'?"

"Traveling."

They stepped onto the elevator. "Poor husband," he muttered, remembering a few of those trips himself. Business travel was lonely.

"I felt sorry for him until I found out about a weekend fling he'd had in Chicago. Then I didn't feel sorry anymore. I didn't even feel hurt. I think that was the beginning of the end."

There was nothing he could say. The car stopped at his floor and he got off, then reached out to accept the other chair. "I'll be right down," he said quietly.

She understood that he didn't want her to come to his place. She handed him the chair and gave a tight nod. By the time the doors whooshed closed, he was halfway down the hall to his own apartment.

THERE WERE FIVE MESSAGES on Duke's machine. Two were from women asking him to escort them to one function or another. Then there was Judy inviting him to a preopening of the new museum, and a message from his son. The last one was from an irate client who was in the middle of an IRS audit and wouldn't be happy, no matter what Duke said or did.

He returned the important calls, picked up his shaving kit and walked out the door. He would handle the other calls tomorrow. Tonight, he was as tired as he'd pretended to be earlier.

When Beth opened the door, he realized he had a skittish woman on his hands. She looked everywhere but at him, and it seemed she was determined to stay at least three or four feet away from him at all times. She began restacking the magazines in a basket by the couch, then fussed with the slipcovers, fluffed the cushions.

They were too aware of each other, and they both knew it.

Putting his hand on her arm, he stopped her just as she was about to disappear into the kitchen. "Let's go back to where we were. Please. Relax. Just because I held you in the moonlight doesn't mean I'm a lecherous jerk. I don't want to throw you down on the ground and ravish your body just because we kissed." *Liar,* a little voice called out, but he quelled it.

She finally looked up and her eyes were wide as saucers. "Why not?"

He would have laughed, except she was serious. "Because you're not ready." He stroked the length of her neck very gently with his knuckles. "And I'm not sure I am, either."

A twinkle lit her eyes. "You don't know?" she asked.

That drew a small smile from him. "No."

A dimple winked in her cheek, then disappeared. "If you don't know, then I'm sure I can't tell you. I just didn't want you to think that a kiss is the same as making love."

"Believe me, I know the difference."

"I wasn't sure. Some men, including CPAs, have a different way of keeping score."

He sighed heavily, then gave a mock warning. "Stop sparring with me."

She grinned, then dropped a light kiss on his chin, which wasn't where he wanted it, but it was a start. "Go to bed," she said. "I'm putting coffee on for the morning."

Neither one moved. "Good night."

"Good night."

As if to prove to both of them that he could kiss her without making love to her, Duke caressed the side of her neck with his fingers and brushed her lips with his. Several times. Beth didn't move, didn't breathe. She couldn't, and neither could he.

It took everything Duke had to drop his hand and step back. He swallowed hard and his throat still felt like coarse sandpaper.

"Good night," he said again, but this time Beth didn't answer. She didn't move as he walked—maybe he ran—to his bedroom and shut the door. All the while he was wondering who the hell's "virginity" he was protecting—hers or his.

For the first time in a long time, Duke McGregor didn't have the answer.

And that made him damn uncomfortable.

5

THOSE TWENTY STEPS between the guest bedroom and Beth's were the hardest steps he'd ever taken in his life. He closed the door to his room with a definitive click and promised himself a cold shower. Immediately. It wasn't an inviting prospect, but it was certainly necessary.

How could a woman he barely knew turn him on so—mentally and physically? How could the woman Benjamin referred to as a "real witch" affect him this way? Was he a glutton for punishment? Was he doomed to be attracted to women who weren't compatible?

He stripped off his clothing and stepped into the shower, shivering in the spray as the freezing water calmed his arousal. The effect wasn't long lasting. As soon as he stepped out, wrapped a towel around his waist, and thought of Beth in his arms, his original problem was back.

All it took was remembering the closeness—that unacknowledged, unidentified tie that silently bound them together and made him feel so damn good. That was his undoing; he wasn't even dry, and his body was as aroused as before.

He threw himself into bed, cursing the whole idea of the rooftop evening. He wished this whole episode had never occurred, then moved on to blame the circumstances that got him to this point. If the furniture company hadn't goofed, he would have been fine; he would never have known Beth or the hold she had on his libido. He could have continued dating and living his life as he saw fit, only including women when he felt the need.

Rolling onto his back, he stared at himself in the mirror above. He wasn't bad looking; he knew that. He kept himself in good shape, working out three times a week, playing racquetball and golf. According to his women friends, he was a fine catch. He had money, a good body and better-than-average looks if you didn't count his broken nose. He looked damn good in a tuxedo. He didn't drink much, had an honest sense of humor and recognized his own abilities. He could live anywhere he wanted and earn a good living on his reputation alone. He drove a Porsche and lived the good life. He'd never beaten his wife. He'd never hit his kid. He wouldn't kick the dog.

And he might have been happy—maybe not happy, but content—with Judy or Faye or Diane, except something else had come along.

He folded his arms behind his head, and muttered, "Something came along. You idiot. Beth came along."

Although he had no commitment to Judy, and having no commitment made it easy to walk away, he knew Judy didn't feel the same way about their relationship. Nevertheless, he'd never led her to believe he was committed, and she recognized and respected his feelings on the subject of "relationship."

His relationship with Beth was a different matter entirely. There were red flags all over the place. His own mixed-up and heated feelings were warning him to be cautious.

He tossed and turned for a while until the sheet was down around his hips. "Damn!" he muttered under his breath as he pulled himself to the side of the bed and sat for a moment. He felt hot. Tense. Awake.

Duke slipped into the worn shorts that had become his uniform here, and quietly made his way to the patio and stepped through the French doors.

As he stood at the railing waiting for his eyes to adjust, he knew before he saw her that Beth was there. He felt her presence. He smelled her. The hair on the back of his neck and arms sprang to attention. He waited for her to speak.

AFTER SLIPPING INTO the new white silk nightshirt she'd bought to match her bed, Beth had tried to sleep. Instead, she'd tossed and turned once too many times. The sensuous atmosphere wasn't conducive to sleep.

Leaving her bed, Beth quietly opened the French doors to the patio. She reasoned that if she was going to be restless, she might as well enjoy the starry night at the same time.

She hated to admit it, but Duke's kiss had wired her body until it hummed. She'd thought all those feelings and emotions were behind her, swallowed up in the divorce. Duke's kiss had proved her wrong. The problem was, she didn't know if she was prepared to bring a man into her life, or even if she knew how. It was time to analyze all those feelings. What exactly was wrong?

Within seconds, she knew the answer. Duke had awakened the hungry tiger inside her, letting her know just how alone she'd felt until now. She'd hidden those feelings deep inside, along with all her other needs.

Slowly, taking a few deep breaths and willing her tense muscles to let go, she began to relax. But then Duke walked out the doors, joining her in the darkness, and she lost ground. It was too late to change into something less revealing than her silk nightshirt, which barely came to her thighs. But determination to wait him out filtered through her. She'd promised herself that she would be true to the *real* her, and that was more important than anything Duke thought of her.

His intense gaze was unfathomable in the darkness.

"Can't sleep?" she asked softly.

"No. You?"

"No."

The midnight sky was a buffer; the darkness gave her the courage to say and do things that were out of character for her. "Do you do this often?"

"What? Sit on the patio in the dark?"

"That, too," she whispered, her voice deep and husky. "But I meant, do you often stay up late?"

He shrugged strong broad shoulders. "Occasionally."

"And this evening? Did I disturb you?" She propped her feet on the railing and pretended she wasn't as aware of him as she was of her own heartbeat.

He wrapped his hands around the railing as if he wanted to choke it. "You do disturb me, Beth. I want you." His voice was as deep as night and twice as dark. "I want you so damn bad I'm gritting my teeth to keep from grabbing you right now and holding on tight."

Her mind went blank when she first heard his words. Then her body hummed in reaction. Her mouth went dry. It took minutes for the rushing sound in her ears to quiet so she could find her voice. "I thought you said you weren't ready," she finally managed. "I thought you really didn't want me."

He turned slowly and stared down at her. "I lied."

"Why?"

"Because you're beautiful, desirable, funny, sexy and..." He let out a breath. "Hell, I don't know. I just do."

"So do I." Her voice was almost a whisper.

He turned to face her and reached out, touching her hair, the side of her cheek, stroking the softness of her skin with his lightly callused fingertip. "What do you think we ought to do about it?"

Beth stood slowly, smiling. "Don't be silly. We both know what to do. We just need to make sure it's really what we both want."

There was no lingering doubt in his voice. "I want. But it's up to you, lovely lady." His gaze was intense, powerful, questioning.

They stood almost touching, neither making a move to be together. He stared into her eyes for what seemed like forever. Then, whatever the battle was, it was over. Softness . . . gentleness shone in his gaze.

"Take me to paradise, McGregor," she whispered.

A grin quirked the corner of his mouth. "How about if I take you to bed first?"

"One step at a time?" she teased with a throaty laugh.

"Just barely. All the books say I need to romance you first. What they don't mention is that I need the romance, too." Duke pulled her head to his chest and encircled her slim waist, holding her as close as their scanty clothing would allow. They stood still for a few moments, loving the silent permission to enjoy the closeness. She felt the heavy thud of his heartbeat against her ear, and loved its strong steady sound.

Then, slowly, Duke began humming a slow ballad, one of her favorite melodies. He kept her body close to his, swaying back and forth, his rock-hard physique against her softness.

She allowed him to lead, reveling in the knowledge that she didn't have to make any more decisions. The most important one had just been made.

Her thoughts faded as his muscles bunched beneath her hands. He bent his head and covered her mouth with his, tempting her slowly, silently into his way of wanting. She craved his kiss, wanted it to go on forever; wanted to let her hands learn him as only a lover could.

He pulled away and traced the outline of her mouth with his thumb. She felt his warm breath on her parted lips and gave a little shiver of anticipation.

Duke smiled. With excruciating slowness, he led her through the French doors and back into the bedroom, stopping at the foot of the draped and canopied bed. He tightened his grip on her waist, then he lifted her up and laid her on the bed. As she sank into the down comforter, it rose around her like a puffy cloud.

This was why she'd bought this bed. Now she had her fantasy in its entirety. Duke and the bed . . . it was like finally completing her personal jigsaw puzzle.

"Ready?" he asked in a husky baritone.

She gave a light laugh. "I have no idea."

"Say no now," Duke warned. "Because, trust me, I won't stop once we begin."

Beth stroked his cheek. "Are you as scared as I am?"

"Yes."

"As nervous?" Her voice was a whisper.

"Yes."

"As wanting?"

"Yes," he breathed on a heavy sigh. "Oh, yes."

Resting her palms on his shoulders, Beth stared at him. With shaky hands, he reached for her silk shirt, then pulled it up and over her head. Moonlight poured into the room and she forced herself not to flinch.

He didn't seem to notice her shyness; he reached out boldly and cradled her breasts in his palms, as if they were pure gold. "So beautiful," he murmured. "You're a wonder."

She stroked the side of his face, suddenly uninhibited, unashamed. Warmth flooded her. Relief. Release. Love. "Thank you."

His thumbs flicked over her nipples, which puckered and flowered for him. Duke bent his head and tasted one, then the other, drawing her breath from her at the same time.

She clung to his shoulders, unable to let go in case she fell off the edge of the wonderful world in which she'd found herself. She felt his muscles flex under her hands as his tongue circled her nipple, and then he suckled her lightly. She'd never experienced anything so sensuous in her life.

His fingers taking the place of his mouth, he pulled away and gazed at her with midnight blue eyes that were hot and intense.

She managed to say, "You're still dressed."

He flicked the button on his shorts, gave a push, and they were pooled at his feet. "Not anymore."

She reached out and stroked him lightly with her fingertips. His instant reaction was all she needed to know. With care, she cradled him in her hand, feeling the thrust and weight of him and reveling in the knowledge that she was the one who had created the need and the proud evidence of it.

He let his hands travel down her rib cage, then come to rest on her thighs. "Silky."

"Strong."

He slid his hand between her thighs and parted her mound. Working magic with his fingers, he watched closely the expressions that flitted across her face. His satisfied smile confirmed that there was nothing she could do but enjoy; she'd reacted instantly.

"Duke..."

"Shh." He placed a light kiss on her mouth. "Lie back. Enjoy me like I'm enjoying you."

"But..."

"No buts," his rough voice commanded. "Do you have protection?"

She shook her head back and forth. She'd meant to get some, but there'd never been any rush. There hadn't been anyone in her life to rush *for*—until now.

"It doesn't matter, sweet." His voice was low and hypnotic, lulling her back into the sensuous cocoon they'd woven. "There's more than one way to make love."

All Beth knew was that having Duke was the only way to ease the ache in her core.

She lay back and he was gone; but then suddenly a wet heat was soothing her, taking away what little breath she had left. She tried to sit back up but his hands restrained her. "It's all right. Relax."

"But . . ."

"I'll be there in a minute," he said, his hands stroking where his mouth had been. "Let me explore you."

"But . . ."

"I want to, Beth. I really want to." Then, with one hand holding hers in reassurance, he continued his foray of her most intimate depths, urging her toward something she'd despaired of ever knowing again.

When it came, the explosion filled her with liquid heat. She arched her spine and then Duke was with her, on her, kissing her as she melted softly back into his embrace. They lay that way—her arms around him, his arms holding her tightly against him. He sheathed himself between her legs, but didn't penetrate her, then began the age-old motion of love. Warmth suffused her. She was grateful. She was content. She was happy beyond belief.

When Duke moaned, she held him close and crooned in his ear until he came back to her from his own travel to the stars. He nestled his head against her shoulder and she continued to hold him, her eyes closed, her breathing finally calmed after the emotional and physical upheaval. He dusted several kisses across her shoulder and she smiled in the dark.

He rolled off her, onto his side, and asked, "Are you okay?"

She touched his cheek. "More than okay."

"Are you sorry?" He stroked her side from her breast to the curve of her hip and back.

She loved the feeling, needing his touch more than she could put into words. "No. Should I be?"

"I hope not. Theatrics and regrets are a waste of time."

Beth tightened her arms around him, realizing that some woman in his life had made him say such a thing. But she refused to ask which one. Instead, she said, "I knew what I wanted. I just wasn't prepared for us to take action."

She saw his boyish grin in the moonlight. "We managed to work it out, Beth. There's no need to be sorry. I don't think either one of us expected this."

Trying to stifle a yawn, she agreed.

His chuckle sounded so warm and intimate. "Come on, sleepyhead. Let's move to the top of this fantasy bed and get some sleep."

Too drowsy and relaxed to do anything else, she did as she was told. Duke went to her bathroom and a few minutes later, touched her with a warm washcloth. Carefully, tenderly, he soothed her.

Except for holding hands across the expanse of mattress, they didn't touch. Beth was afraid to get any closer in case he read her as being needy or wanting to make love again. This was all so new that she didn't know what to do; all she knew was what not to do. She couldn't let him know how welcome he was. It would be too forward. Besides, she was perfectly capable of sleeping without a man in her bed, and nothing had changed.

She closed her eyes and told herself to fall asleep right away. And she did.

But somehow, in the middle of the night, she awoke to find herself curled within the shelter of Duke's arms, her head resting next to his on the same pillow. They were smack in the center of the bed, having drawn close together sometime in the night. She blinked once, twice, smiled, then closed her eyes again. She was exactly where she wanted to be. Duke didn't seem to mind, either.

DUKE WOKE UP BEFORE dawn and stared down at the woman curled against his side. He knew immediately where he was and who he was with. There was no guesswork.

That didn't mean he waived all regrets. Hell, no. He wished more than anything that he'd had the good sense to stay out of Beth's fantasy bed last night. He hated long goodbyes and sticky, complicated affairs—and he had a feeling this relationship could turn into one or both of those if he wasn't careful.

Duke remembered his son's comments about Beth and realized that, at times, even his kid had more sense than he did. This wasn't a move to take lightly. He should have planned ahead, taken it one step at a time so either one or both of them could have bowed out when they felt threatened. The way he did now . . .

He gently removed his arm and slid off the bed. Still asleep, Beth sighed and reached out, and he rested his hand on hers before backing off. What he wanted most right now was to get out of here and have some breathing space, some room to think. When he was around Beth, reason flew out the window and the urge to make love took over.

As quickly as he could, he gathered up his stuff and left.

BETH HEARD THE FRONT door click and knew that Duke had left. Gone instantly was the feeling of contentment and peace she'd experienced all night long. Funny. She hadn't felt used until just this minute.

Obviously, she wasn't good enough for him. He was wealthy, and wealthy men usually went for young trophy wives. Well, it was for certain that Beth wasn't one of those.

No. And surely he was looking for someone less family oriented, some swinging single—someone like Judy, the woman he'd just broken up with.

Beth sat straight up in bed. Good grief! She, Beth, was the rebound woman! He'd been so upset about losing the woman he wanted, that he'd rebounded straight into her arms!

Damn!

Sliding out of bed, she went immediately to the shower. Of course. That was it. She was second choice. Good grief. Why hadn't she seen it coming?

Well. When—if—she saw him tonight, she would be cool and calm and pretend that nothing had happened. She wouldn't be too far off, and no doubt, according to Duke McGregor, not much *had* happened.

Otherwise, he would have stuck around to say good-bye instead of fleeing as if the female equivalent of Attila the Hun was after his handsome bod.

"To hell with him," she said, putting an end to that.

SUSAN CAME INTO his office late that afternoon, carefully closing the door behind her and sitting down in front of his desk. "Well, do you want the bed moved day after tomorrow?"

He looked up from a tax report. "Why?"

"Because I found a bonded moving company who could do it right away."

Duke was disappointed; he wasn't ready to leave Beth's place. All day long he'd avoided making the decision, knowing he would have to do it sooner or later. He'd chosen later.

Tossing his pencil on top of the report he was editing, he stared hard at his secretary. Something was up and it wasn't about this decision. But she wouldn't tell him until she was good and ready. "How much do they want?"

She told him the price. "But both you and Mrs. McGruder have to be home in order to have it moved. It's a small company and they need supervision in order to comply with their bonding company. So, *she* has to be there when they tear it down and *you* have to be there when they set it up at your place."

He was relieved. This was his perfect excuse. "Then forget it. Mrs. McGruder can't take time off work unless I pay her, and she won't let me do that."

"What makes you say that?" she asked, curiosity piqued.

"I already tried to reimburse her for letting me stay in her apartment. She refused. Twice." He remembered the twinkle in her eye at the time, and a small grin quirked at the corner of his mouth.

"Interesting." She stood. "So you want me to do nothing until the furniture company can move it next week?"

Duke picked up his pen and pretended to resume editing the report in front of him. He could feel the knowing look in his secretary's eyes, but he sure as hell wasn't going to glance up and confirm it. "That's right."

"Oh, one more thing," she said before she got to the door. "Judy's been cooling her heels in your waiting room. Should I send her in, or give her her walking papers?"

Duke sighed. "You're going to be the death of me." He was now resigned to the fact that his secretary was at war with whoever she'd decided was the enemy. He couldn't blame her; she'd been provoked by Judy's superior attitude the first time they'd met. Susan never forgot or forgave. "Send her in."

Susan snapped her fingers and made a face. "Darn."

Duke couldn't help the grin that forced its way out. He'd been working with Susan for six years and she always knew what to do to make him ease up.

A MOMENT LATER, Judy saw the remnants of his smile and relaxed instantly, walking toward him with the grace of a confident predator. "Well, Mr. McGregor, I see you're in a good mood. I hope my being here has something to do with it."

"This is an unexpected visit, Judy. How's everything?" he asked cordially, staying on the other side of his desk. She walked around the desk and kissed him in a way that was more than friendly.

Duke pulled away and stared down; his smile had disappeared. "What can I do for you?"

She glanced at him coyly, as if to say he knew what she wanted. He returned her look with a blank stare. He almost felt sorry for her, although in all the time they'd been dating, he'd never led her to believe she was the only one. If he was the only man in her life, it had been her choice. Still, he felt guilty for leaving her in the lurch.

She sighed. "I know you're busy, but I was in the neighborhood and needed to ask you a very important question." Her eyes were wide with concern. "I have to attend a function at the museum this Friday evening and I wondered if you would escort me. It's too late for me to find someone else."

Duke understood. They'd only broken up last week and she'd been out of town since then. She hadn't had the chance to let her social group know she was available.

His hesitation must have been apparent. "Just as friends, Duke," she coaxed. "I promise."

"It'll have to be an early night. I'm visiting my son this weekend," he warned.

Her smile was relieved, but beautiful as she was, she just didn't call to his libido like Beth did....

"Thank you. Early is fine with me, too."

After she'd left, Duke sat and tried to understand what it was about Judy that *didn't* turn him on. For the life of him, he couldn't put his finger on it. She was single, successful and would be a great asset to his business. She was also earthy and, occasionally, fun. Yet Judy didn't make his heart beat faster and Beth did. It didn't make sense, but that was the reality.

Images of Beth had been popping into his mind all day long. He worried about how she'd felt, waking up to find him gone. Had she realized he'd had to get ready in a hurry, or did she think he'd just escaped an awkward situation? She deserved more than some guy slipping out the door after a night of making love...their first night.... For the first time in his life, he felt bad for doing what came naturally. He picked up the phone and dialed her number. The answering machine came on.

"Look," he said, speaking onto the tape, "I didn't mean to leave so abruptly this morning, but something came up and I had to attend to it immediately." *Liar*, he thought. "I'd like to make amends by cooking dinner for you tonight. Something simple, believe me. If it's all right, give me a call on either phone when you get this message. I'll look forward to seeing you." He gave her the phone numbers she needed and hung up.

It was amazing how good leaving that message felt. It took away the bad taste that had been in his mouth all morning. He tried to reason out the how and why, but finally gave up. "Too much introspection is a bad thing," he muttered to himself, getting back to the report on his desk.

It seemed that as time went on, life became more complicated. Sometimes he wished he'd become a psychologist.

"MR. MCGREGOR?" Beth's daughter exclaimed incredulously. "Good grief, Mom, you don't mean he's actually *sleeping* there!"

"Yes, that's exactly what I mean," Beth stated calmly, not feeling at all the same on the inside. "I told you one of my neighbors was staying for the night."

"I know, but you never said his name! I can't believe it! He's such a chauvinist! And his son is such a geek!"

"That has nothing to do with this, Cassandra. I have Mr. McGregor's bedroom set and the furniture company can't move it to his apartment until next week. Letting him sleep here is the neighborly thing to do." She didn't mention going to bed with the man and making mad passionate love to him, which was also neighborly, she told herself.

"Well, just remember, Mom. He's the devil incarnate, or so Benji says."

"I thought Benji was a geek."

"He is, but he used to sit behind me in geometry class and sometimes we'd talk." Her daughter hesitated. "He was better in geometry than I was, so he helped me on occasion. But he was *still* a geek." Her tone was defensive and emphatic. "And even he said his dad was the devil!"

"I'll bear that in mind," Beth stated dryly, letting her daughter know how much she valued "Benji's" opinion.

"One step at a time," she told herself. Then she marched to the bathroom and began the process of applying makeup. If nothing else, she was going to knock Duke dead in his tracks with her beauty. He would be so captivated he would be her sheikh "slave" for life.

What was she thinking? Just knowing they'd made love last night and she was going to see him tonight, made her feel awkward. She was like a teenager again, giddy with happiness and nervousness, and full of the fear of being rejected.

THAT NIGHT BETH SERVED broiled lemon chicken, several vegetables and crusty sourdough bread, topped off with a crisp white wine. They ate on the patio so they could view the sunset.

She'd accepted Duke's invitation to dinner by countering with one of her own. He accepted her offer without a moment's hesitation, which told her he was using dinner as an excuse to get together earlier than bedtime.

They chatted while she prepared dinner, each carefully avoiding the topic of last night and their lovemaking. They talked all through the meal, both sharing details of their lives and routines in an easy friendly way. They went on talking as he puffed away on a small cigar.

She hadn't felt such ease and companionship with a man ever before.

Much as she pretended otherwise, Beth recognized deep down that she would never have gone to bed with Duke on a whim. She wasn't the type. And yet she didn't want to admit that she cared more than she should, either. But he was so gentle and sensitive.

When she'd been slicing vegetables, she'd cut her finger.

"Let me see," he'd said, taking her finger and staring down at the cut.

Beth had felt the heat of his touch all the way to her toes and had wanted to reach out and run her fingers through his hair.

"Beautiful palm," he said softly, once he'd examined the cut and decided it must be okay. His thumb stroked the center of her hand.

It was hard to find her voice. "It's no different from anyone else's."

His blue-eyed gaze captured hers as his thumb kept stroking. "How do you know? Do you make a habit of comparing women's palms?"

"No." She wet her lips. "Do you?"

He nodded solemnly. "It's my duty to do so. Yours is by far the most beautiful."

"I'm impressed by your expertise."

There was a glint of humor in his eyes. "I'm impressed by your . . . impressions."

"Smart aleck. You're just saying that 'cause you want to ravish my lithe and sensuous body."

"You're right and you're right." He brought her palm to his lips and caressed it with his mouth.

Beth wished she could laugh it off, but she couldn't. She could hardly find her breath, let alone the part of the mind that dealt with laughter, or speech. "I, uh, I . . ."

"You want to take me to bed and ravish my body?" he suggested.

"Yes."

"You want to tease and taunt me with delights only heretofore known in the great harems of the East?"

"Yes."

"You want me to help you clear up the dishes first?"

At the mention of cleaning, the fog began to clear. "Yes." She laughed. She had to—he was so damn *cute!* "Come on before I change my mind and decide that dishes are all we can do together." She took her hand away, stood and started to stack the plates.

"You mean we can still do what *I* had in mind?" He followed her lead and began gathering up the condiments.

"As long as you do a good job cleaning up."

"Believe me, with incentive like you, my mother could have gotten a whole lot more work out of me."

"With incentive like me, *I'm* hoping to get a whole lot more work out of you." Her tone was dry, but her smile refused to be squelched.

"I promise," he answered solemnly. "I'll try hard all night."

A flash went off in her memory of all the times early in her marriage when she'd been asked to drop the housecleaning and run to bed to play. But concern for the children or the dread of doing later what could be done now had always rung the bell of responsibility.

"Then let's start now," she said, for the first time in too long ignoring the responsibilities of life and the kitchen. She held out her hand to him.

And he took it.

She led him into the bedroom, then turned, pinning him between the bedside and her own slim body.

His eyes widened.

She smiled and gave him a knowing look. "Your turn to undress first," she murmured, slipping his shirt buttons from their holes. When she reached his waist, she pulled the tails of his shirt out of his trousers. After that, she tugged at his alligator belt, then undid the snap of his waistband.

Duke stood very still, watching her every movement, his hands resting on the high bed. When his pants fell to the floor, he smiled. "Is it my turn, yet?"

"No," she said, answering his look with one of her own, not knowing where she got the nerve to continue. "We've just begun."

With smooth motions, she stripped the shirt from his body, then took off everything else until he stood naked, his growing need obvious to both of them.

"Now, me," she said in a husky voice. With deliberately slow movements, she began unbuttoning her shirt, then removing her straight skirt, and eventually she stood dressed in only a black bra and thigh-high hose. She knew from the look on his face that she made his temperature rise—she looked sexy.

"Now, teacher?" he asked in a husky voice.

"Not yet," she said, but he paid no attention.

He came toward her, determination etched in his features. "Too late," he said, "I'm taking you now." He picked her up and placed her on the high bed. "If I weren't so damn horny, we'd be in *my* bed right now, playing out *my* fantasy."

She circled his neck with her arms as he joined her. "Tough luck," she whispered in his ear. "I acted first." Her tongue flicked his earlobe and she felt a shiver go through his body. "So it's my way...."

"And my way," Duke whispered back, before capturing her mouth with his and making her forget whose bed and whose fantasy they were in....

6

HALF AN HOUR WITH JUDY at the museum party, and Duke was ready to drop her off and head back to the peace and safety of his own home. Or Beth's arms. That admission, though quietly made, was a relief. It was a relief to admit that he felt as if he'd known Beth all his life, and still couldn't learn enough about her.

"What do you think about this one, darling?" Judy's voice interrupted his thoughts.

They hovered in front of a canvas that was larger than his patio and consisted of a splash of red paint. "I think it stinks." This wasn't his kind of exhibit. Come to think of it, these weren't his kind of people, either. Moreover, Judy kept trying to make them seem like a couple.

"Let's cool this lovey-dovey stuff, Judy," he finally murmured as they strolled away. "We're not a couple anymore, and I wouldn't like to give the impression that you were taken. After all," he said, "any of these eligible men might like a chance to meet you if you were free."

"I've never been free and you know it." She chuckled conspiratorially in his ear. "And don't patronize me, darling. I already know who's looking and who's not. I also know that I'm already head over heels in love with you, and nothing you say is going to change that, so you might as well get used to my adoration."

"It's not going to work."

"Not if you won't give it a chance."

"I'm not interested," he stated. "You know that already."

She refused to accept his candor. "Oh, you're interested, all right. But you're even *more* scared, so you run in the opposite direction."

"You've got quite the healthy ego, Judy. I'm amazed, actually. I didn't realize anyone could be so self-centered."

"Don't kid yourself, Duke. Everyone is." She gave a casual shrug. "And why not? I knew your wife and she was far worse than me. You ought to be thankful. At least I'm better for our social life and career."

"I don't have personal relationships to further my career. And I'm out of that greedy way of life. I'm happy with the way things are."

"You just think you are," Judy said confidently, as if she knew him better than he knew himself. That assuredness had drawn him to her in the first place, and it was the same attribute that now turned him off. She never stopped to think she could be wrong, or that other people's feelings might be at stake. "I'm capable of making you more content than you are alone, Duke, and you know it. You're just afraid of a repeat performance of your past marriage. I promise you that ours won't be that way."

"And how can you promise me that?"

"We're compatible in many ways. Same friends, functions, same sexual drive. Same sense of humor."

She was almost right. "There's one thing missing, Judy. The rapport that comes from being on the same wavelength. It isn't there for us."

Judy stopped in front of a Renoir and fixed her gaze on it. "You're heartless, Duke," she said at last. "If you wanted to, we could make it. But you want to throw away all the good things between us."

"Don't cry now," he mocked, knowing she couldn't have been further from real tears. "I'm sure someone else will make that magical connection with you. You're beautiful and intelligent. Most men would be in awe of what you have to offer."

She finished the unspoken part of his sentence: "You're just not one of them."

"Unfortunately, no."

"Too bad." She took his arm again and they walked farther down the line of paintings. "You don't know what you're missing."

"I think I do. I'm just choosing to miss it."

"I wonder how different it would be if you had your bed in your own home?"

"How did you know about that?"

"I sat cooling my heels in your reception area for almost half an hour while Susan tried to find a company to move it. I heard most of the gory details."

Duke smiled and took another glass of white wine from the floating waiter. "There's no need to get nasty," he said, wondering how he could cut the eve-

ning short so they wouldn't get into a full-fledged
brawl. There was another couple approaching them
so he murmured, "Let's be friends and not draw
blood."

Judy went on tiptoe and kissed his cheek, then blew
delicately in his ear. "If you say so. You're the leader,
darling. I'm just along for the ride."

Somehow he doubted that.

WHEN HE REACHED BETH'S door, he felt as if he was
home.

He slipped into his shorts, then found Beth on the
patio sipping a glass of tea. He sat down with a sigh
that spoke of how glad he was to be there.

"Tired?" she asked.

"No, just relaxing from a rough day and an even
rougher evening." He gave her a smile and she smiled
back, warming him far more than the wine could ever
do.

"You're all scrubbed and ready for bed," he ob-
served.

"Like you, I want out of the rat race for a while. I
came home early to lick my wounds and hide from the
world until tomorrow night."

"Tomorrow night? What's happening then?"

"I'm attending a party in my old neighborhood. It's
the Morgans' anniversary." She sipped on her wine,
not looking at him for fear he would see the raw emotion she felt when she was near him. "Want to go?"

"Thanks, but no thanks." He laughed, easing back in his seat once more. For a moment he'd thought she had a date. It was her business, of course, but he wouldn't continue bedding any woman who was sleeping around. At least, that was the excuse he was using for the quick spurt of jealousy that had jolted him. "I'll be at A&M with Benji."

"Oh, that's really nice," she said, her tone bland, as if she didn't give a damn about his whereabouts. She could have acted like she cared just a little.

He knew better than to voice that opinion aloud. He would sound too possessive. And possession went both ways. He wasn't ready for that—and never would be.

They talked about their work, about the kids and what they wanted to do the next year. Duke enjoyed the evening so much, he realized that this was where he belonged—with Beth—at least for right now.

When it was time for bed, they went together to her fantasy bed. Tension sang between them.

"Want to try mine?" he asked, spanning her waist with his hands.

Her soft laugh delighted him. "Your what?"

"My bed," he clarified. "We haven't tried it yet."

She cupped his jaw with her small hand. "I'm not mentally prepared to be seduced by a throwback to the sixties."

"And what's this bed like?" he asked, turning out the light and joining her on the playground-size mattress. He lay back and she curled into his arms, resting her head on his chest, light-as-air fingers touching him. "This is definitely a sixties fantasy, Ms. Mc-Gruder."

"That's just it. This is a fantasy of seduction."

"You're splitting hairs."

"Of course. It's the subtleties in life that count. And you, Mr. McGregor, need to learn them. That's why women were placed here cn Earth—to teach you unenlightened men the difference."

"I know, I've heard it before. I'm a man and I ought to be whipped to pay for the sins of my sex."

She gave his chin a kiss. "I'm so proud of you. See how much you're learning, already?"

He chuckled. "You're one righteous mama."

She tried to stifle a yawn. "And don't you forget it."

Two minutes later, Beth was sound asleep in his arms.

In the middle of the night, he awoke and turned hungrily toward Beth's warm body. She came to him easily, willingly, and they made love with slow, gentle movements that spoke volumes of tender, heartfelt words. Then, still silently, they entwined limbs and fell asleep once more.

DUKE AND BENJI SAT in the box-seat section of Kyle Stadium on the Texas A&M campus and watched the marching band perform with geometric precision.

"So I told her, she'd just have to find some other guy to wait on her, hand and foot. I wasn't it." Benji reached for another peanut to shell. He'd just given

Duke the rundown on his latest exploits with women. It wasn't a long list, but it certainly was angst-filled.

"Are you sure that's what she wanted?" Duke asked, trying to keep the conversation open.

"First she asked me to move her into another apartment, then she wanted me to help with the decorating, then it was a loan for a new stereo. Does that sound like the woman needed more TLC than the ordinary?"

Duke had to stop and think for a minute. Just two weeks ago, he would have agreed immediately. But slowly, and with the influence of conversations with Beth, he was learning what life was like on the other side of the fence. It wasn't easy for a woman to get what she needed. "Sometimes that's a woman's way of asking you to share her life."

"Sounds more like she wants me to be her slave," Benji said disgustedly. "Everything was pointing to her wanting me to do the dirty work around the house."

"Are you saying she should do it all?"

"Well, no," Benji drawled, but gave his dad one of those looks that said he would do as little as possible.

"I hope there's a time when you do more than your share, son. In a marriage, as in any other relationship, sometimes you have to step in and help when you least want to. But further down the line, when you need help, you'll have it."

"Are you my dad?" Ben teased, but then he looked solemn. "I know what you're saying. It's just that I'm

not sure her motives are as pure as you're suggest-
ing."

"Cut her a little slack. She's just trying to get you
involved. You might find that giving a little doesn't
hurt as much as you think. If I'm right, you'll get back
a lot more than you bargained for."

"What's the matter, Dad? Getting a little soft in
your old age?"

"Only a teenager could say that and get away with
it," Duke scoffed. "Maybe I am. And just maybe that's
not a bad thing. Being strong and silent isn't necessarily the best way to be in your personal life."

Benji's smile dropped, and he looked puzzled. "You
always said to go after what you want, then hold on
to it and ignore everything else. You said that was how
success was born."

"And I'm still saying so. Just remember that a
woman isn't an 'it,' son. And that very same woman
may give you the most wonderful moments you'll ever
have in your life—and I don't mean in *that* way."

Benji grinned. "Gotcha, dad. I'll think about your
words of wisdom." He paused for a moment, looking
at Duke with an air of wonder. "Who would have
thought you'd get so smart when it came to women,
seeing as you were married for so long?"

"And married men don't pay attention to what goes
on in the world?"

"Well, I guess my thinking was wrong," Benji admitted a little sheepishly.

Duke knew when to close his mouth, and now seemed as good a time as any. They cheered the team and stood and yelled and gave the proper hand signs. But all the while, he wondered what Beth was doing. He knew she was at a neighborhood party. Was his name being bandied about? Was someone making a pass at her? Did she wish he was with her?

He wasn't sure where this relationship was leading anymore. In the beginning it was just a fling; Beth was simply a nice woman whose company he enjoyed. But he wasn't seeing anyone else, and he suddenly realized that this was the first time he'd been away from her and that he missed her—a lot.

Duke shook off his thoughts. He wasn't looking for commitment and marriage, and he was sure that Beth was the marrying kind. He wasn't ready for that, and maybe he never would be. He needed to make sure Beth understood that.

Just the same, he wished he hadn't promised to stay in town and have breakfast tomorrow with a bunch of Ben's friends.

He wished he was going home to Beth. Leaning back, he let his mind wander. Quickly enough, he was back to the question foremost in his mind: What was she doing?

THE MCGRUDER TWINS stared at their mother in shocked disbelief.

"He's *still* staying *here? In your home?*" Cassandra's voice rose to a disbelieving, high-pitched whine. "Mom! How could you?"

"How could I what?" she asked, propping her feet up on the coffee table. She'd always liked putting her feet up, but she hadn't done it until she'd gotten a place of her own. A place her ex-husband didn't remind her of the hard labor it took to buy things. She thought about that with a smile on her face. Somehow that didn't seem so bad compared to her daughters giving her grief over the man who was sleeping in the spare room.

"Mo-ther," Carol cried. "How can you stand that man in your house?"

"Are you saying that because he's Benji's father?" Beth asked.

Cassandra dropped dramatically into the overstuffed chair across from her mother, her eyes wide. "No!" She looked scandalized, then intrigued. "Does Daddy know?"

Beth felt anger scratch her soul. She gave her daughter a look that she hoped said it all. "Is it his business?"

Carol sat down on the floor, her back to the footstool. "Well, I guess not, but it's kind of odd, you know. Him being Benji's dad and all."

"And I'm not supposed to have contact with anyone from my past, is that it?"

Their mother's dry sarcasm finally reached them. "Are you angry, Mom?"

Beth took a deep breath in an effort to get her temper under control. "Yes. I don't see why anyone, including you two, should have anything to say about my life unless and until it has to do with you. And in that case, I will have the courtesy to tell you myself. Immediately." She gave both her daughters stern looks. "Otherwise, what I do is my own business, unless it somehow interferes with your life."

"We just don't want you hurt, Mom. You're not quite savvy in the ways of the world, you know. Sometimes I think we know far more than you do."

"I can manage, dears. Believe me, I'm not naive. I just don't choose to share my knowledge with you on this particular subject."

"So you wouldn't have said anything if we hadn't asked?"

"I wouldn't have, except it would have been a little hard to hide the fact that he's occasionally here when you're going to be sleeping in Mr. McGregor's bed tonight."

"Well, gee, Mom," Cassandra said, her feelings hurt. "You don't have to get huffy about it. We just found it hard to believe that Mr. McGregor, who spawned Benji, was involved in your life."

"Yeah, Mom. We were just concerned. That's all."

"Well, I appreciate your concern, but please don't worry. Mr. McGregor will have his bed back by next week and everything will be back to normal."

Both girls looked doubtful, but neither forced a confrontation.

Beth understood just how difficult it was for them to let go of the image of their mother as a helpless woman who wasn't able to make a decision without checking with their father first. It had taken Beth time to get used to that, too. But she'd been divorced almost three years and it was about time the girls updated their image of their mother. No time like the present.

Although she wasn't in the mood, Beth went to the Morgans' party and socialized with friends she'd known for years. The wives were as fun as always, the husbands as solicitous as ever. But as the only single there, Beth felt out of place. It reminded her of how it felt to be part of a pair, and there was just a little nostalgia in the reminder. Still, she appreciated the fact that her friends thought enough of her to invite her to functions like this. It made her feel like a valued friend. Too bad Duke hadn't been there with her. . . .

She quelled that thought. Duke had made it plain he wasn't looking for a long-term affair. It didn't matter that she cared more than he did; she would just enjoy the moment. Her heart knew better, however.

Her daughters also went out that evening, club hopping with friends, they'd said. Returning home before them, Beth sat back and thought about how much her life had changed in the past few years; she'd become a single woman and her family had grown up.

By the time she heard the girls open the front door, Beth was in bed, attempting to sleep. They burst into her room, bounced on the bed, curled up beside her and began telling her all about the old high school friends they'd run into.

"And then I just happened to mention that Mr. McGregor lived upstairs from you. And you know what she said?" Cassandra's voice rose to a crescendo. "She said he was a foxy guy! Can you imagine?" She laughed.

Carol looked shocked. "Can you imagine?" she echoed. "I thought I'd die! I said, 'Do you remember Benji and how dorky he was?' And she said, sure, but he was cute about it. And then she said his father wasn't the only person who had to do with his creation, and she said maybe Benji's mother was just a tad weird." Carol looked at her mother inquisitively. "Do you think she was weird, Mom? She always looked beautiful to me. Don't you think she was svelte and beautiful?"

Before Beth could answer, Cassandra did. "And I always wondered why she left him. Or did he leave her? What went wrong, do you think, Mom?"

"Think there was another woman?" Carol asked. "Who do you think it was?"

Beth had her daughters' complete attention, and she was speechless. Had it not occurred to them that their father was one of those men who had met their new wife while their old wife was still a wife? Did they not understand how much this conversation hurt?

Of course not, she answered herself. They had no idea, and she wasn't going to be the one to tell them. She took a deep breath. "I think she is beautiful, although I haven't seen her lately," she said slowly with a smile. "And I don't know if there was anyone else involved in their breakup and wouldn't have the nerve to ask. And yes, it takes two to make a child, just like it took two of us to make you lovely women."

"Do you think we're more like Dad?"

"No." She was forceful on this point. "You're like me. You don't distrust everyone who comes through your life, thinking that someone might take advantage of you." She hoped that was true. She had tried so hard to change that part of her emotional makeup.

"Yes, but Carol isn't as open with people as I am."

"That's because she's shy, not because she distrusts everyone."

Carol nodded. "That's right. It's not the same thing."

"And what did we get from Dad, then?" Cassandra demanded impatiently.

"Your impatience," Beth said dryly, and both girls laughed.

They continued to talk until almost three in the morning, and Beth enjoyed every minute of it. It reminded her of days gone by, when the girls were younger and the world seemed, if less happy, also less complicated.

By the time the girls sleepily made their way to Duke's bed, Beth was exhausted. Still, she remained wide-awake, her mind going around and around like a squirrel in a cage as she realized how lonely she was without Duke.

Tonight's party, the children, all the introspection . . . all the events of the evening, had brought her to a realization—she was in love with Duke McGregor. And there was nothing she could do about it. It wouldn't do to tell him, to let Duke know or to whine about it. It was just a fact, and that was that, because it was obvious he didn't feel the same way or she would have known it.

Thank goodness that, curled in her fantasy bed, she didn't find it hard to imagine Duke beside her, or she might never have drifted off to sleep. The rest of the night was spent in dreams in which Duke was happy to be with her.

DUKE AWOKE BLEARY-EYED the next morning. He sat at the table with five young men Benji's age and listened to more sentences containing "you know" and "man" than he'd ever heard before. It didn't matter that he'd known half of these boys since his son was in first grade; it was as if he was seeing them for the first time. They were a good group of kids—nice young men. He only hoped that time would give them the polish needed to make it in the world. Right now, Benji seemed like the most responsible one of the bunch and the glimmer of leadership Duke saw in his son made him proud to be his father. If nothing else, this morning was giving him a glimpse of what lay ahead.

Okay, he told himself, *I learned what I was supposed to learn on this trip. Now I can get back to Beth.*

He stood and reached into his back pocket for his wallet.

"What are you doing, Dad?" Benji asked, a fork filled with waffle halfway to his mouth.

"I'm leaving. It's time I got back."

The boys protested, but Duke smiled, gave his son a hug, and waved goodbye as he strode out the door.

His duty was done; now he could move on to something just for him.

BETH DREW ONE LAST frustrated breath and fantasized about a secluded convent in the north of France, where no one could get to her except on alternate Thursdays—maybe. By Sunday morning, the girls were packing to return to Austin, and it wasn't a moment too soon. Beth was ready for a little peace and quiet. Her own chaotic thoughts were enough to cope with right now.

Just as the girls brought their luggage out of Duke's room and dropped it in the entryway, the doorbell rang.

"I'll get it," Cassandra called, flinging open the door with her usual enthusiasm.

"Hi." The sound of Duke's voice seemed to singe Beth's nerve endings. "Is your mother home?"

"Oh, uh, sure," Cassandra muttered, her gaze holding a surprised and wary look.

Duke made it halfway from the door to the couch and stopped. He stood between the two girls and Beth. "Hi." His smile was broad and only for her.

"Hi." She couldn't keep the happiness out of her voice.

Cassandra and Carol stood expectantly in the doorway, silent for the first time all weekend. Their blatantly inquisitive gazes brought Beth back from her fantasy of fitting into the welcome curve of Duke's arms.

One of the girls moved toward the kitchen and Duke looked over his shoulder. Their curiosity was evident. "I'm sorry. I didn't introduce myself. I'm Duke McGregor." He turned and stepped forward, shaking hands with each of them. "I believe I've seen both of you, a long time ago."

"Of course," Carol murmured, always polite.

"Really? I don't remember," Cassandra said with a toss of her hair. "But if you say so . . ." Her voice dwindled off as she caught her mother's expression. She snapped her fingers as if her memory had suddenly awakened. "Oh, wait. Of course! You're Benji's dad, right?"

Duke played along. "That's right."

"How is Benji? I haven't seen him since we were kids!"

Beth kept her smile in check. "Kids" was last year at graduation.

"He's doing fine. I just came from having breakfast with him and a few of his friends." Duke glanced at Beth, giving her the reassurance she needed to know that he wouldn't hurt her child's ego with careless words—even if she *was* acting like a pill right now.

"As a matter of fact, he'll be on your campus next week. He's escorting a girl to a sorority dance."

Cassandra looked surprised. "He is? Which sorority?"

Duke told her and her eyes opened even wider. "That's a great one," she enthused. "You can't pledge for it until you're a sophomore and have proved yourself successful on campus. And your grades have got to be top-notch."

"Really," Duke said, as if he hadn't known.

Beth realized he'd known exactly what he was doing all along. He'd won the girls over—at least to his son's advantage—just by presenting the right image. Amazing.

Carol came to Beth's side and gave her one last hug. Cassandra followed suit. Then they picked up their overnighters and opened the door. "Tell Benji to look us up when he comes into town. We'll buy him a cappuccino at our favorite hangout and introduce him to a few friends. He'll remember some of them from school."

"I'll tell him," Duke promised.

Then they were gone.

"They're good kids." Beth said the words with a trace of humor. "They're just a little protective."

Duke didn't let the space between them remain empty. He closed in on her and enfolded her in his arms. "'A little' is an understatement," he said, before dotting kisses across her cheek. "I think I've collected at least a thousand daggers in my back."

"A slight exaggeration." She lifted her head to give him better access to her throat as he trailed kisses in that direction. "But whatever wounds you have, I'll make them better."

"How?" he murmured, sliding his hands down to caress the swelling fullness of her breasts.

"I'll give you a massage cheap."

"How much?"

"A thousand dollars a minute. The full treatment is at least an hour."

"I want it all."

Her mind was fogging up. Every nerve sang, begged for him to continue. Never to stop.

"What else does the full treatment include?"

She could barely get the words out. "An open bottle of wine, a few dozen candles and my precious time."

"What? No chocolates? No peeled grapes? No pomegranates or apricots? What kind of a harem is this?" He reached under her T-shirt and felt the weight of her breast, palming it gently before circling her nipple with his thumb.

"The best kind." She sighed in soft relief as his hand cupped her possessively. "I know what I want, and I've already asked for it."

"May I return for a night of decadence in a few hours?" he asked, his voice as ragged as her nerves.

She shook her head, trying to clear the sensual haze. "What? Why?"

"I have to hit the office for a few hours. I'm meeting a new client in the morning and I promised I'd have the presentation printed out for him."

"Now?"

He pulled his hand out from under her T-shirt and kissed the tip of her chin. "I know. I'm insane. But I really don't have any choice. If I don't go now, I'll have to leave after we make love. And I wouldn't want to do that."

She smoothed her hands over his shoulders. "You're right, but I'd like to hang you from your thumbs for starting something you knew you weren't going to finish."

"Lord, I love the nineties." Duke chuckled. "Women can finally be honest and say what's on their minds. Forget being coy and childishly sweet about making love."

"*This* woman," she corrected softly. "Don't compare me to all the other women who float through your life."

"You're right. You're—" He stopped himself and pulled away. Beth had the feeling he'd just slammed a door that she wished was still open.

"Go. I'll keep my, uh, heart in the drawer until you return," she stated dramatically.

"Sounds painful." He stared down at her. "You'll still be here in a few hours?"

"Yes."

She saw his shoulders relax. "I'll be back. Promise."

Beth reached up and kissed him lightly on the lips, resisting the urge to hold on and keep him there. It wasn't right to let him know just how much she cared; he wasn't for her for always. Just for now . . .

He was heading out the door when he turned back and said, "By the way, what did the girls think of my bed?"

"They thought you were decadent and shouldn't be allowed anywhere near their saintly mother."

"Well, they're half right," he muttered. "God bless our misguided children," he said, and closed the door.

Beth lay down on the couch and closed her eyes. Her daughters' visit had left her drained. She needed a catnap.

Maybe two minutes later, she heard a key in the lock, the door reopened and Duke stepped in. She knew it was him, although she remained on the couch, her eyes still closed.

His kiss was light, sweet.

"Mmm," she said, her eyelids fluttering open. "Is that you, Mel Gibson?"

"Why, how did you guess?" he asked, a hint of laughter in his voice. "To hell with work. It can wait until later. I've decided to ravish your body instead. It's the least I can do for such a desirous woman."

"And they say you're all brawn," she drawled.

"I'm that, too," he responded, shrugging out of his jacket and lying down beside her. "That's why you're so crazy about me."

"You're right," she said softly. "You're so very right."

"Come on. I want to play sheikh."

Beth giggled. "If you insist, master," she teased, then scooted even closer to him. "But don't you think we ought to move to the bed?"

"Definitely. Eventually."

Duke gave a sigh and captured her lips with his.

To hell with the paperwork . . .

7

WEDNESDAY, DUKE HAD a golf date with one of his most demanding clients, Dr. Samuel Samson, who lived for the game. Unfortunately, it didn't help his handicap. He still played lousy golf.

The good doctor had made his millions when he'd helped build a local hospital, years ago. That same hospital ended up being sold for an all-time record-high price to a conglomerate. Samson and his fellow investors were suddenly very wealthy, and now relied on Duke to keep them on the straight and narrow with the IRS. It wasn't always an easy task. The doctors were behind the times by thirty years, and Duke had to treat them carefully while bringing them into the nineties with all the new laws the decade had produced.

Although the dues were stiff, Duke had joined the country club early in his career and had seen the advantages of being a member. He sometimes thought more business was done on these grounds than in all the offices across this section of sprawling Houston.

Today, Samuel had brought two of his cronies along, Morty and Charlie, and they played nine holes in easy quiet. It wasn't until they reached the tenth hole that the conversation moved into personal territory—or as personal as it ever got between men.

"So, Duke, who are you seeing this month?" the doctor asked, giving a wink to one of his older colleagues. Samson had always been interested in what he called "the swinging life" and Duke had a feeling that during those moments of conversation, the doctor was living vicariously through him.

Before, Duke had usually obliged by exaggerating his exploits with the women in his life. Not that he put them in a bad light; just a little sexier and more "saucy," as the doctor was fond of saying.

This time was different. This time, Duke didn't want to talk. He didn't want to discuss his personal life or let anyone know about Beth. At the same time, he was so damn happy, he could have shouted about their relationship from the top of the tee box.

Duke took his time setting up the next shot, then performed beautifully, hitting it to the next green to sit five feet from the hole. "No one in particular," he finally hedged, putting his club back into the bag. His caddie, a young high school kid, wore a grin as large as his face.

"Man doesn't play golf that well unless his love life is in order," Charlie said.

Morty was carefully lining up his shot. "Man doesn't do anything well unless he's got a good woman in his life," he muttered, hitting the ball directly into the woods.

Duke laughed. "You're *all* cynics."

"We may be," Samuel stated. "But we're right. Come on, 'fess up. Who is it?" Before Duke could answer, Samuel went on. "It can't be Judy, unless she's changed a hell of a lot. Besides, you played golf with me three weeks ago when you were seeing her, and that was your worst game yet, as I recall. Nothing like today."

"Worst compared to what? Yours?" Duke continued to walk down the fairway toward the next shot. It was Morty's ball, just a dogleg off to the right.

"Worse than your usual worst. And don't hedge. Come on, tell the doctor everything or I'll start billing you for your visits."

Duke laughed. He wasn't going to answer except that he was curious to hear what these guys knew about Beth. "Judy and I aren't seeing each other anymore. I'm not really dating anyone, but I do see Beth McGruder occasionally."

Samuel looked shocked. His usually half-closed lids flew open. "Beth McGruder? Stan's wife?"

Duke felt irritation rise and barely kept it out of his voice. "Stan's *ex*-wife. And yes, *that* Beth McGruder."

Morty squinted and looked through the woods, trying to locate his ball. "Cut it out for a minute while I make this shot." He shuffled his feet to get the proper stance, took another look, readjusted his feet, then finally let one fly. It soared hard and fast—right into a tree at the edge of the wood, bouncing to the ground not ten feet from where they stood.

Morty gave a heavy sigh, then led the parade to the second location. "Beth McGruder. Isn't she the blonde with the sweet smile?" He shook his head. "I used to love to watch her walk across the country-club parking lot in those short-shorts."

"You've got sex on the brain, Morty," Samson complained. "And at your age it could get you into trouble or the hospital. Either one."

"I could get into trouble at any age," Morty retorted.

Morty settled his stance over the new lie, gave his butt a slight wiggle, then hauled off and swung. Duke could have sworn he closed his eyes. His ball landed smack on the green about fifteen inches from Duke's.

"Knew I could do it if I concentrated," Morty stated confidently.

"Don't get involved with a woman who might still love her husband, Duke," Samson warned. "You don't know how often these divorced women look sweet, then turn on you when you least expect it, going back to their husbands and whining about the men they were with during the breakup. It's sad." He shook his head as if he'd never heard such an awful thing before.

The good doctor had been married for over forty years, and unless he'd fooled around on the side, his experience with divorced women was limited. Duke would bet that despite his talk, the doctor had never cheated on his wife. He adored her. "Run into a lot of them, have you?" Duke asked dryly.

"Every day." Samson shook his head as if he were talking about a deadly virus. "It's so sad. No matter the reason, they can't seem to pick themselves up and begin again. Their identity's all wrapped up in the ex-husband, and everything they do is measured by that yardstick."

When they hit the green, Samson was still warning Duke. "Stay away from that Beth, son. Find yourself some sweet young thing and train her right from the beginning," he whispered. "That way, she'll know just how you like things and make sure they stay that way."

Duke gave a sigh and silently admitted that the three men weren't playing with a modern deck. They were stuck in a time warp.

While that old-fashioned philosophy was fine for them, it wasn't right for Duke. He would go nuts with some woman simpering over him. He wanted someone who had a life of her own; someone with a strong sense of herself and her place in the world. He'd married a woman like the ones they were discussing and the marriage had failed after just a few years. They'd just waited until the children were grown to bury the relationship.

"Thanks for the advice," he said quietly, knowing it had been given with good intent, even if it was useless to him. He'd already decided he had to stop listening to everyone else and follow his own voice telling him what was good for him. After all, who better to know what Duke McGregor needed most than Duke McGregor? And Beth was high on his list....

One small thought nagged at him. *Did* Beth still want to be with Stan McGruder? She refused to say anything bad about him, and he'd assumed that meant she was a balanced, stable woman. But maybe it meant she was still secretly in love with her husband.

He hated how much the very thought hurt.

Later in the day as they headed toward the eighteenth hole, Morty leaned over and imparted yet more advice. "Get yourself someone wild and willful in bed. In the long run, that's where the fun is. You won't remember all those television shows where you sat and held the wife's hand, and if push came to shove, you could probably live without her meat-loaf surprise. But if she slipped off her nightie and gave you a wink, you'd remember that, my boy."

"I'll keep that in mind," Duke replied, then stroked his ball into the cup for a birdie.

They were walking toward the clubhouse for a drink at the end of the day when Charlie leaned over Duke's shoulder and spoke into his ear. "Find a woman who can cook and wants to stay home. Those others will tug on you and whine, when all you want is to eat a decent meal and fall asleep in front of the TV. It's important to get someone who's compatible."

Duke thought so too, although his idea of compatibility had little to do with sitting in front of a TV.

Thanks to these guys, he'd suddenly realized just how young and virile he was. As his son laughingly referred to him, he was a "happening dude." He was in the prime of his life, and it was high time he started enjoying it.

And what he would really enjoy more than anything else would be to hold Beth for a few minutes, maybe an hour. He didn't have to make love to her, just as long as he could hold her and feel their closeness....

BETH AND LINDA MET for lunch and a movie—a romantic comedy.

"Why can't men be as romantic as the ones in the movies?" Linda complained. "If my husband ever kissed my hand or whispered sweet nothings in my ear, I'd swoon."

"Frank does pretty well," Beth countered, not allowing her friend to lose sight of her husband's good points. She'd known them both since their children were little, and she liked Frank. "Besides, he doesn't have to whisper anymore. Your last chick has left the nest—he can shout if he wants to."

Linda giggled. "And he does! Last week he shouted downstairs, 'Linda, get up here! I've got the bathwater just the way you want it and if you don't get in here with me, I'll pop every bubble!'" She laughed again. "What he didn't know was that the next-door neighbor was standing in the doorway handing me our paper, which had been dropped in their yard by mistake."

Beth laughed. "What did you say?"

"Not a thing," Linda stated complacently. "I just watched the envy grow on that woman's face." She sighed. "I'm lucky and I know it. I just like to grouse a little."

"Well, take it from me, you're lucky."

"You need someone in your life, Beth," Linda began earnestly. "Someone to fuss over. Heavens, you don't even own a cat!"

"I don't want a pet, Linda, just in case you think you're going to pawn one of your animals off on me." Beth warmed to her subject, for the first time putting words to her previously unspoken desires. "If someone is going to be fussed over, I want it to be me. *I* want to be the one who feels treasured this time around."

"Well," Linda said, grinning. "It seems the lady has discovered what pleases her. Anything else?"

"Quite a few things, actually, but I'll leave them for another time." She thought of Duke, and knew one of her fantasies would be to find him in her bed, ready for long, slow, lovemaking when she got home.

"Sure you don't have anyone in mind for all this love and attention?"

Beth felt her cheeks redden, but she remained calm. "Of course not. Otherwise I'd be with him instead of you, right now."

"So," Linda said softly. "There *is* someone. I knew it. You can't lie to me, Beth McGruder. You always look away and down when you're lying or stretching the truth. 'Fess up. Who is it? Anyone I know?"

Beth tried to casually explain the mix-up with their beds and the fact that Duke was staying at her condo. She didn't mention that he spent more time in her bed than he did in his own. She didn't have to.

"Wow!" Linda exclaimed. "As much as Frank is my stud muffin, Duke McGregor is stud with a capital *S*."

"You know him?"

"I know *of* him," Linda replied. "He runs one of the largest accounting firms in the city, and he's been on every charity board that's ever been created." She gave Beth a knowing look. "I work for a CPA myself, remember? Our firm isn't in the same league as his, though. We cater to personal accounts, while he's into the corporate stuff." She looked hard at her friend. "So? Are you going to tell me more or not?"

"Not," Beth said. "There's nothing more to tell. The furniture company called and said they'd be moving the bed in the next few days. Duke threatened them with a lawsuit if they didn't, but you know how that goes. They've been promising that forever. But they're going out of business. They don't care."

"And neither of you are that anxious to do anything about it," Linda guessed correctly.

Beth decided to face it head-on. "Would you be?"

"Do you love him?"

"Yes."

Linda smiled broadly. "Does he love you, too?"

Beth took a deep breath, raising troubled eyes to her friend. It felt so good to finally talk about it. "He hasn't said a word. I haven't got a clue."

"Really? His reputation in business is that he's very up-front, so I'd imagine he'd be the same way in his personal life."

Beth's spirits plummeted even more. "If that's the case, then he's not in love or he'd have said so by now."

"Have you told him how you feel?"

"Of course not."

Linda shrugged. "Well, then, why should he tell you?"

Beth had to laugh. "We're not teenagers. I can't send a friend over and ask him if he likes me. And I certainly won't tell him myself. If he's not interested, I'd look like the world's biggest fool."

"Somebody's got to give in," Linda stated reasonably. "It might as well be you."

"Hold that thought," Beth said, "but don't hold your breath."

For the rest of the afternoon, Beth's imagination taunted her with the thought of Duke returning home. Had things changed? Had he met another woman in his absence? Had he changed his mind about having her in his life? He was so solicitous, so kind. So giving. So *single*. It was an attitude he had; it reminded her constantly of just how single he was. She had the feeling he withheld an intimate part of himself from her—perhaps from all women—so he wouldn't become too emotionally involved.

She prayed she was wrong, but she didn't think so. Even when they'd shared those many conversations deep into the night, Duke had kept an emotional distance between them.

When they parted, Linda gave her hand a squeeze and vowed loyally, "Don't forget, Beth, you're worth two of any other woman he could find in his life." She added, "And it's very possible that he's in love with you, even though he breathes more rarefied air than most."

"Thank you, I think," Beth answered with a resigned sigh. Linda was only voicing Beth's own fears.

"Look, I know this sounds weird, but as much as I want you to go for the gusto, I also don't want you to get hurt again. And Duke McGregor is a man who could hurt you. Deeply. Be careful." Linda's concern was real.

So was Beth's.

She *could* get hurt. But it was too late for her. She was crazy about the man and was willing to ride with him on this roller coaster going nowhere—at least for a while.

WHEN SHE ARRIVED HOME, Mrs. Rutgar stuck her head out the door. A spry smile lighting her eyes. "Your beau just arrived," she said, "loaded with groceries, so I think he's planning a surprise dinner for you."

Beth's key remained in midair. Her heartbeat quickened at the thought of him just on the other side of the door. "In my apartment?" she asked.

Mrs. Rutgar nodded. "Have a nice evening, dear," she said, then shut the door quickly. Beth heard the latch slide into place.

She opened the door and walked in, slinging her purse over the edge of the couch. "Duke?" she called, noticing he wasn't in the kitchen or on the patio. She looked toward his room. "Where are you?"

"I'm in the bedroom," he called. "Come here."

Her first impulse was to tell him to come to her, instead, but she thought better of it. She walked quickly to her bedroom door and opened it.

Duke stood, legs braced and hands on his hips at the patio door, dressed in white and looking every inch the master of a harem. On the bed was a large silver tray holding a champagne bottle, glasses, a bowl of fruit and an array of cheese and crackers.

Her heart thumped heavily in her breast. A slow smile lifted the corners of her mouth. "Lawrence of Arabia, I presume?"

His grin was wicked. "The Sheikh of Araby," he said, bowing deeply. "At your service."

"Is that whip for looks or do I have to run for my life?" she asked, her voice sounding breathless even to her ears.

He took a step closer. "Have no fear, my dear. I would never harm a hair on your head." He kicked the door closed with his foot. Then, with a narrowed gaze, he came toward her and wrapped his arms around her waist, slowly pulling her to fit closely against him. "However, this room is your prison for the next twenty-four hours. Your fate is sealed. You can enjoy it, or not. It's up to you."

She wrapped her arms around his neck and smiled beguilingly. "Help, help," she whispered. "Rescue me."

"I will," he said just before capturing her mouth in a kiss that melted her heart.

He was her fantasy. She ignored the wish deep in her heart, that he was more than that.

THE FURNITURE COMPANY called with two dates when they could move the bed—next week or the week after. Beth chose the week after, using her unavailability as an excuse, weak as it was. Duke agreed.

She wasn't sure *why* he agreed and she was afraid to look too closely for fear she would find indifference. Although he didn't act indifferent, she was suddenly unsure of everything to do with Duke.

She knew, in her deepest heart of hearts, that once the bed was gone, their relationship would dwindle away. She couldn't take that chance without trying, in this one last week, to make him care about her the way she cared for him. Loving him too much, aching to be with him too often, Beth refused to give up even the slightest contact until she had to. If she could put off the bed moving, she would. And after that, she just didn't know.

She was impatiently waiting for a miracle.

The next week, Duke spent every evening with her. He called out for dinner twice, made dinner—and a big mess—once, and savored her home cooking three times. On the seventh night, he took her to a popular steak house he liked.

They took a seat by the wall, where large plants provided a privacy screen between them and the front door.

Beth's smile was contagious, and this evening promised to be as much fun and just as heady as all the others they'd shared. He refused to think about the fact that he was falling in love.

He preferred to call what was going on inside him "chemistry." As long as his feelings were couched in that noncommittal language, they were acceptable.

"My goodness! Honey, look who's here!" Suddenly, Kay stood there, her eyes as large as the salad plate in front of Beth.

Duke glanced across the table. Beth looked as if she had the same plate embedded in her throat.

"Beth!" Kay exclaimed. "How good to see you out on the town without all the rest of us!"

"Hi, Kay. How are things?" From Beth's smile Duke knew she felt the same way he did—disappointed that someone had broken into their idyll.

"Great. The real-estate market is going so well, I'm swamped with listings. Luckily, my other half got me out of the house before I quit my job and ran away to join the Foreign Legion!"

Beth laughed. Kay was funny, sweet and kind. "I'm sure things have been hectic."

Kay looked pointedly at Duke. "Aren't you going to introduce us?" she asked, wrapping her arm around her silent "honey" and looking expectantly at Beth.

Beth waved toward them, then Duke. "Kay, Gene, meet Duke McGregor."

Duke stood, holding his napkin while he shook hands with Kay's silent partner. "Are you part of the crowd who meets once a week to go wild?"

Kay looked delightfully surprised. "Why, yes. How did you know?"

"Beth told me about you all. It seems a once-a-week get-together is a carved-in-stone ritual. She really enjoys it."

"I didn't know she even discussed us." Kay looked charmed. "And how long have you been in the picture?"

"Long enough to know about your meetings," he said, giving her a lazy smile.

Her grin widened. "I didn't know she was seeing someone special." Kay's gaze darted to Beth. "She never said a word."

Duke didn't know whether to be pleased or slighted. A little doubt niggled at him. He wanted Beth to be proud of him, to be so captivated by him that she couldn't help but talk about him. Hell, he'd done it with his golf buddies. Which reminded him...he was supposed to be careful. "Well, it hasn't been that long since our first...date." He gave Beth an adoring look, laying it on thick for Kay. "And you know how shy she is about her private life."

Beth's gaze hardened to diamonds. "Really, Kay. There's nothing to tell."

"Doesn't look that way to me," Kay replied, taking in more than Beth wanted her to know. "But we won't keep you. If I don't put something in Gene's stomach, he turns into a tiger."

Beth had a hard time conjuring up that image, but if Gene turned into a tiger for Kay, that was all that mattered. "Well, I can certainly understand that. No man should be without his evening meal, especially when he's got a beautiful woman by his side."

Kay picked up quickly. Duke hadn't finished his salad yet and the entrée was surely on the way. "See you later," she said. "Maybe we can have dessert together."

"Another time." Duke's tone was regretful but firm. "We're making it an early night."

When her friends were out of earshot, Beth speared a tomato chunk. "Thank you," she breathed, looking as if she'd been holding her breath ever since her friends had joined them.

"For finding privacy or for being kind?"

"For both. You could have been a diplomat."

Duke's grin was unrepentant. "I was good, wasn't I?"

Beth's dimple showed. "You did your mother proud."

"So you weren't anxious to have them join us?"

"No. Kay's a dear friend but I see her once a week. I don't see *you* nearly enough."

"You've seen me almost every evening for the last couple of weeks."

"Really?" Beth popped a wedge of cucumber into her mouth. "Are you keeping track? Should I feel offended or flattered?"

Duke's next words surprised both of them. "How about treasured?"

She put her fork down slowly, staring at him with more tenderness in her gaze than he'd ever seen before. He felt bathed in it and it was the most wonderful balm in the world. "When you look at me like that, I could climb Mount Everest if you asked me to."

Her mouth tilted delightedly at the corners. "Why would you want to do that? I had no interest in going that high."

"How high are you going?"

"Only as high as you'll take me." Her voice was low, but he heard every word, watched her full lips move as she spoke.

He took in her delicate features, his gaze brushing her eyes, her mouth, her peach-tinted cheeks. He felt his throat go dry with desire. "How do you do this to me?" he finally growled. "Just when I think I've figured you out, you have me reacting like a schoolkid."

"Once a minute?" she teased.

He covered her hand with his, feeling the warmth emanating from her and wishing he was covering more than her hand. He nodded. "At least. Be grateful I've learned how to control myself, or I'd be making love to you right here and now on this table."

Her gaze widened. "And whose fantasy is that?"

"Mine. Now."

She dropped her gaze, then looked back up with clear and direct eyes. "I thought your bed had said it all. I guess I was wrong."

The waitress came and set sizzling steaks in front of them. "Saved by the food," Duke murmured. "But when it's gone, I'll still be hungry."

"Don't mistake your feelings," Beth warned.

"Not a chance. Not tonight."

Beth stared at him. Then her smile widened, delightfully crinkling her eyes at the corners. "If you insist . . ."

"Behave yourself or I'll do something drastic right here in front of the waitress and everyone." Duke's voice sounded gruff even to his own ears, but Beth didn't seem to mind.

She sighed and leaned back, palms up. "I give. You win. We'll go home and try out your fantasy bed."

"But first I get a long, toe-touching, soul-searching, time-consuming body hug. Right?"

Her laughter refreshed his soul. "Right."

Duke paid the bill and they left the restaurant with a wave toward Kay's table. Holding hands, they walked slowly to the car, enjoying the cooling breeze and the scent of fresh pine.

They drove the few blocks home with the car windows down. Once he'd parked the Porsche inside the garage and helped Beth out of the low-slung seat, he pulled her into his arms and leaned against the car, giving her one of those hugs they'd talked about earlier. His hands resting on her hips, he let a deep, wonderful, relaxing sigh escape his lips.

BETH WAS FEELING MUCH the same way until a memory intruded. She suddenly remembered seeing another woman in this place, in Duke's arms, and her heart tightened in her breast. She didn't want another woman to ever be in this place again. She wanted to be the only one who had the right to stand this close to the man she loved.

There it was. The words didn't flit by. No, they took root in the front of her mind, where she couldn't ignore them. She knew, as she knew nothing else, that this love would hurt and thrill her like no other. And it was out of her hands.

She looked up at him, memorizing his features as if she might never see him again. With one finger, she traced the strong line of his jaw, the arch of his eyebrow. A deep sadness fell over her like a dark cape.

Duke took her finger into his mouth, sucking lightly at the tip as he watched the parade of expressions cross her face, leaving her with sadness in her gaze.

She had to shake it, had to get rid of this feeling. If their relationship wasn't to be, she would have plenty of time to plumb the depths of her misery further down the road. But not now. Not when she could be enjoying this time.

She cupped his face in her hands and smiled. "You know what you need, mister?" she asked throatily.

He nodded. "I need you to put me to bed."

She laughed. "Eventually. But right now, you need to put on some shorts and go for a walk along the golf path."

"Now?"

She nodded. "Are you game?"

He didn't hesitate. "If you're going, I'm going."

Beth broke away, took his hand and began running toward the elevator. It felt good to move, to have some control over her actions even if she had none over her feelings. "Last one to the elevator's a rotten egg!"

"Last one there is you!" he shouted, running toward the elevators like a kid in a race.

Beth felt him gaining on her as she flung open the stair doors and ran up, two at a time.

Duke took the elevator, laughing all the way, thinking he'd won.

He was wrong.

8

THEY WALKED BRISKLY along the narrow track that edged the residential road. It felt good to move, to feel the cool, evening dew against her skin. Most of all, it felt wonderful to have Duke holding her hand in his as if he wouldn't let go.

"Do you do this often?" he asked, breaking the silence of the past five minutes.

"Often, but not often enough," Beth said. "I used to walk through the neighborhood every evening after dinner, in my old home. I miss having a little land, working in my garden. I miss not having a place where I can sit quietly at night and stare at the stars."

"You have a balcony."

"It's not dirt. It's not plants and trees." She took a deep breath and glanced around. "It's not private."

"They why didn't you stay in your old neighborhood?"

"I couldn't afford it. Not on my salary. I also realized that my ex-husband's promise to help me keep it together for the sake of the girls wasn't going to last past his memory, which seems to be shorter these days than ever."

"So you made the logical decision to give up that way of life, even though you loved it?"

"It wasn't that easy. But you know how it goes. Your wife chose to stay in the family home and you got all the obligations."

Duke gave a sound that might have been agreement. Beth had a feeling she was bringing back more thoughts of his previous marriage than he wanted to deal with right now. She tugged on his hand. "Come on. Let's jog."

They did—for all of four minutes. Beth quit first, and Duke was obviously relieved by her decision.

"Where do you get your energy?" he asked, standing with his hands on his hips as he tried to catch his breath.

"If I had any, I would have beat you into the ground," she finally found the breath to say.

His laughter cut through the night air and warmed her insides with its rich, deep sound. He led her over to a bench near a tee box. Beth sat curled against his side, her feet propped up on the bench. Duke's arms encircled her from behind.

"It's midnight." His voice was low, sexy, and definitely carried more of a message than the words implied.

Beth's heart skipped a beat. "Will you turn into a pumpkin soon?"

"I'll turn into a knotted ball of nerves if you don't take me home, give me a large glass of water and put me to bed—next to you."

"In a minute," Beth promised, unwilling to let the night end yet. She stretched her legs out and snuggled into Duke's arms, reveling in the peace of the moment. Her hands covered his, resting on her stomach. She soothed the fingers, stroked his wrists, touching in a slow and easy rhythm that matched the night.

Slowly, she felt him begin to unwind. It wasn't often he let go of that uptight, inner caution and allowed himself to ease up. But when he did, she felt happily responsible for it. He needed to do so much more often.

Standing, Beth left the comfort of his arms and scooted around behind him. Duke looked over his shoulder. "What are you doing?"

"Don't worry. I won't hurt you, big boy. I'm just going to take some of the tension out of your shoulders." She placed her palms around his neck and began kneading his thick, bunched muscles.

"You can hurt me all you want, honey," he drawled, "if this is your definition of the word. In fact, why don't we go home and you can *really* hurt me?"

She tightened her hands. "Watch it, buddy. Stop the innuendos and try to do as I say for a change."

"Sorry," he said, unrepentant. "I'll relax."

"Take a deep breath, then let it out slowly."

He did as he was told and more tension left him. She began kneading his muscles again until she'd eased out all the knots. Then she sat back down in the curve of his lap, giving his arms a light squeeze as she pulled them around her once more.

Duke kissed the top of her head. "Why did you do that?"

She lied. "To make you wait so you'd get good and sexy."

He didn't buy it. "Why?"

She sighed and tilted her head to stare up at the almost-full moon above. "Because you're always so controlled and tense, even when you're relaxed. I just wanted you to enjoy the evening as much as I am."

"Is this one of those 'Life is too short to be unhappy and tense' speeches?" His tone held a distinct hint of ridicule.

"You bet. Have you heard it before?"

"Yes."

"And you decided it wasn't true? You'd rather be unhappy and tense than happy and relaxed?"

"Of course not."

"Then what?" she challenged.

Duke thought for a moment, and gave her a reply that she knew was a brush-off. "You're making life much more simple than it is, Beth," Duke responded, irritation lacing his voice.

"What's not simple?" she persisted. "You're in the middle of life right now. Either you enjoy it or you don't. If you don't, you'd better change something or you'll never enjoy it. You'll never find happiness in the things you do."

"Do you enjoy cleaning the oven?" he asked.

"No, but I make darn sure I enjoy the results. Besides, you haven't named something I absolutely hate to do. Life's too short to expend that much energy on hating something that doesn't take very long."

"You're an optimist."

"Optimism is a learned trait. That's been proved."

Duke's laughter rumbled against her back. "You're nuts, do you know that?"

Satisfied by this concession, which told her he couldn't keep up the tough exterior forever, she patted his hands. "Yep."

Silence sat comfortably between them. Duke sighed. "And you're probably right," he admitted.

"Yep."

"I'll try to enjoy life more. I promise."

"Yep."

"As soon as my next business trip is over."

Beth found her voice with effort. "When is that?"

"I leave tomorrow."

Her heart sank. "For how long?"

"Four days. I have a client in Austin and he's got some problems he thinks I can solve."

She didn't want him to leave. She didn't want to wonder who he was with and if he was having a good time. It was a strange thought. She'd never bothered to be jealous before. Was she so unsure of this relationship that she couldn't trust him? "Why doesn't your client come here?" The words were spoken before she could withhold them.

"He's a congressman who's fast becoming a millionaire. He doesn't have the time."

"Is he honest?"

"I have no idea. All I do is figure his quarterly taxes and handle his retirement fund."

"And you don't know?"

"No. Everything's done and my office merely inputs data already completed."

"If you found out he was cheating on his taxes, would you drop him as a client?"

"Of course," Duke replied, his voice filled with surprise. "What the hell do you think I am? I'm not losing my career for anyone. I'm good at what I do and I do it legally. That's why I get paid so well."

She felt better, but for the life of her, she didn't know why. Maybe it had something to do with the idea that if he cheated in business he might cheat in his personal life, too.

He'd said no.

But her first fear was still sitting like a rock in the pit of her stomach. Only one more week before the bed was moved. One more week to spend with Duke, and then his bed would be gone and everything would be back to the way it was before. Because of this trip of his, she only had three days instead of the seven she'd anticipated....

She didn't want their growing love to die.

That shadow was on her spirit again. She stood and stretched out her hand. "Come on, big boy. I know where there's a big glass of water, a hot shower and a soft bed. You look like you could use all three."

"Thanks, I think," he said dryly, accepting her hand and standing.

This time they strolled back to the tower alongside Cypress Creek. This time, they kept their arms wrapped around each other and stopped occasionally to stare at the stars. This time they showered together.

And this time, as always, Beth tried to show Duke just how much she loved him with every stroke, touch and kiss.

THE NEXT MORNING, after a wonderful night of lovemaking, Duke left. They went out the door together, greeting Mrs. Rutgar through the gap in her chained door as they walked toward the elevator.

Beth pushed the button and Duke reached for her, pulling her into his arms for one last kiss. "I'll be back before you miss me," he whispered in her ear.

"It's too late. I miss you already."

A low ding echoed through the hall, announcing the elevator. "I'll see you Friday," Duke whispered in his husky voice.

"I have a dinner appointment. I'll be back around ten-thirty," Beth answered. "You've got the key. I'll see you then."

"Take care."

She stepped inside the elevator and the door closed, shutting her off from Duke. With the creak of wires and the whir of a motor, the elevator headed toward the parking garage. Beth blinked several times, wishing away the dark feeling that was closing over her. She felt so very alone, and that scared her.

Until Duke, she'd been content. What was that old saw? *I was my own best friend, then you came into my life and put me in second place.*

"Come back to me," Beth said aloud.

But Duke couldn't hear her. He was upstairs in his own condo, packing for a four-day trip that wouldn't end soon enough.

TWO DAYS LATER, Beth was glad that Duke wasn't around, for the moment.

She'd walked into her home to find Cassandra on the couch, wrapped in a blanket. Her face was a pasty white against a mass of long blond hair, but the blaze in those young eyes was enough to light the furniture on fire.

"What are you home for, honey?" Beth asked, dropping her purse and going over to feel her daughter's forehead. "Don't you feel well?"

"I'm sick."

"Since when?" Beth asked, feeling the hot dry skin against her hand.

"Since yesterday. Brandon drove me home."

"Why didn't you call me at work? You have the number." Beth stood and draped the afghan over her daughter's exposed feet. "Did you take anything for the fever?"

"Yes, about half an hour ago." Cassandra's voice was strangely cold. "I think I've got the flu."

Beth wrote it off to the illness, and went to get a cool, wet washcloth.

She put some extra pillows behind her daughter and then, with slow strokes, wiped her face and neck.

"Did you call the doctor?"

"I went to the campus infirmary this morning, and they gave me antibiotics, just in case." She motioned to the small prescription bottle on the coffee table. "I took my first dose about three hours ago."

Beth repeated her ministrations. "Have you eaten?"

"No. My stomach's too upset." Cassandra leaned back and gave a hearty sigh. "I can't believe it," she finally managed to say dramatically. She closed her eyes and allowed a tear to leak through.

Beth knew that aside from the flu, she was dealing with some other crisis in her young daughter's life. "What can't you believe, honey?"

"You. My own mother." Cassandra's mouth twitched as if she was going to burst into tears.

Beth became alarmed. "What's the matter, honey? What's making you so sad?"

"Mom . . ." Cassandra's voice ended on a hiccup. The floodgates finally opened and she began crying, clinging to her mother's shoulder. Beth rocked and crooned to her daughter, as her mind skipped from one thing to another and she tried to figure out where to lay the blame for this upset. Nothing seemed to fit.

"Is there some man out there who needs a set-to, honey?" she asked. "Is that what this is all about?"

Her daughter nodded against Beth's shoulder.

"Do you want me to go out there, find him and kill him slowly? Or should I just mess around with a cat-tle prod for a while?" Beth teased, relieved that it was only a man and not some terminal disease.

"I don't know. Do you love him?" Cassandra's voice was muffled against her shoulder, but Beth didn't miss the meaning.

But she asked for clarification, anyway. "Who?"

"Duke McGregor."

Beth pulled away slowly, looking down at her daughter. "What about him?"

Cassandra looked up at her mother with accusing eyes. "You let him sleep with you, don't you?"

"Yes."

"In your bed!"

So that was it. "Why would you even ask?"

"It doesn't matter. I know it's true. I went into your bedroom and saw his shorts on the floor! You *slept* with him! Mom, how could you do that?"

"No, you misunderstand me," Beth stated quietly. "I was being rhetorical when I said why would you ask. I meant, Where do you get the nerve to ask what goes on in my home? Who I spend my time with is none of your business until I decide to make it your business."

"Of course it's my business!" Cassandra exclaimed. "You're my mother!"

"Did you ask your father these questions? I think not. And I don't deserve them, either."

"He and his wife weren't sleeping together before the marriage!" At Beth's incredulous look, Cassandra lifted her chin defiantly. "At least they were in a committed relationship!"

Beth took a deep breath and tried to hold her temper in check. "Neither your father's relationships nor mine are any of your business Cassandra. If you hadn't come home, you wouldn't have known anything about my dates or my friends until I'd decided to tell you. And we wouldn't be having this conversation."

Her daughter looked shocked. "Are you saying this fling with Mr. McGregor could be serious?"

"I'm saying that this conversation is over. I'm not going to answer any more questions about my personal life. If you need anything else to make you feel better or more comfortable, all you have to do is ask. But Duke McGregor is none of your business."

With careful precision, Beth stood and left the living room. She went into her bedroom and closed the door behind her, leaving her daughter on the couch with her mouth open in astonishment.

Beth leaned against the door, her nerves wound so tightly, her body shook. Her children had no idea how hard she'd fought for some sort of identity after the divorce. She'd had to discover what her tastes were, who her friends were, and how she reacted to things without input from her mate. It had been hard and scary and wearing. It was just as hard, scary and wearing to have a relationship, which was why she'd retired from the dating game. It was just too hard on the ego and the emotions. There were plenty of women who were better looking, younger, smarter, sweeter, less apt to give a comeback off the top of their head, and certainly others had more charisma than Beth could ever claim.

So why had she become involved with a man who was all the things she wasn't?

Why had she fallen in love with that man—the very thing she'd sworn never to do?

She knew she was on the way to Elvis's Heartbreak Hotel. Even her daughter saw that.

Yet, she wouldn't stop riding this roller coaster of love until the trip was over. As for her children, they went about their own business without much input from her—until something in her life was of interest to them, and then they butted in.

This wasn't their business—which wasn't to say she didn't care about them and their opinions. It just meant there would be no more judgment calls. She and her girls weren't playing the same game on the same field and didn't know the rules for each other's lives anymore. It was only fair that Beth called the shots in her own world—with or without her children's permission.

She took a deep breath and pulled away from the door. Heading toward the closet to slip out of her work clothes, she realized that she felt this nerve-racked because she had no more of an explanation for her relationship than her daughters did. She had no idea what Duke felt for her. She'd been too afraid to ask.

AFTER TWO DAYS of rest and stilted conversations with her mother, Cassandra felt good enough to return to school. Beth was as relieved as Cassandra when they parted with hugs and love between them.

Although she told herself otherwise, Beth had a niggling fear that Cassandra might be right—that Duke was not for her. The thought ached so much, she shoved it to the back of her mind and tried to forget about it. Time would tell, and soon enough she would have to deal with Duke's leaving. Soon enough...

That evening, the night before Duke was due back, Beth had dinner with Stan. They'd planned it over a month ago, and now the time was here, Beth was nervous. They needed to talk about the college funds and the school year ahead. But after the past few days with Cassandra, Beth had to wonder how much the girls had said to their father about her. She wasn't sure she wanted Stan to know what was going on in her own life. After all, he was with someone else now, and they had both buried their share of hurt and guilt over their marriage's demise.

They met at a small Italian restaurant. Neither shook hands, neither kissed a greeting; just smiles.

"Hello, Stan. You look good." He looked like hell, actually, with dark circles under his eyes and a paunch defining his waistline.

"Thanks, so do you."

She had lost four pounds but was wearing a five-year-old dress that he'd seen plenty of times before. She sat down and quickly glanced at the menu as the waiter hovered. "I expected your wife to join us," she said.

"She has a family function tonight. Besides, this is about our children, so I don't see a need to drag her into this."

Beth smiled. "Don't get defensive on me, Stan. I was just making an observation."

Stan ruefully acknowledged her mild admonition. "To tell you the truth, Beth, I haven't seen you in almost two years and I didn't know what your attitude would be, so I'm a little nervous."

"So am I," she admitted, finally relaxing. They could handle this. They'd eaten a thousand meals together before. They'd been polite before. They could do this. "What say we both relax and get through this with as little pain as possible?"

"That would be nice—and different," he replied, and he said it with a smile.

The conversation was general at first. They talked about friends they'd seen and business people they'd known. Stan told anecdotes and Beth laughed. Beth told of the girl's first days at college and related a few of the funnier frantic phone calls, and Stan laughed.

It was strange, but maybe because they weren't pressed into being together anymore, much of the emotional strain between them was gone. The divorce was final, the settlements were complete. It seemed as if they'd both decided to make the best of the situation.

She couldn't have been more happy. After all, she'd originally found the man worthy of marrying. Just because they hadn't made a go of their marriage didn't mean he was scum; it meant they could no longer live together and be happy.

"Beth?" Stan's smile drifted away. She'd seen this expression before and knew he was going to give her something to think about. "What happened to us? Where did it go wrong? Do you know? I sure don't."

She reached for her wineglass and twirled the stem, struggling to find the words that she needed. "I'm not sure, but I think we both stopped trying. We forgot to touch each other. We forgot to talk. Even to laugh. We forgot to work as hard at *us* as we did at the rest of our lives."

"We certainly worked hard once."

She nodded. "Yes, but somewhere along the road, that changed. Everything became more important than our marriage."

"You're not blaming just me for all our ills anymore." He made it a statement.

Beth couldn't help a smile. "No. And you're no longer accepting all the guilt and then lashing out at me for it."

Stan leaned back with a sigh. "No. I only got angry because I knew how you felt about that emotion. It was my way of striking back, of pushing your buttons. We both had some problems communicating."

"Darn," she said softly. His look was startled. "Here I thought I had you pegged as a scapegoat for this

failure of a marriage. Instead, you insist on shoulder-
ing only half the blame."

The grin he gave her never reached his eyes. "I think
my share is more than half but less than whole," he
amended. "Why didn't you tell me how bad it was
getting?"

"I did. You just didn't want to hear it." She leaned
forward. "But we're not here to dig up a dead marriage. This was all buried a long time ago. You have a
new partner and a new life."

"And an old failure."

"And two girls who love you as only daughters can
love their daddy. I just want to make sure that you and
I don't stunt that growth. The men in their lives will
be very important, and you're the most important
man of all. You're actually their link to the future
spouses they choose."

"A heavy burden." Stan raised an eyebrow. "Another lecture?"

She didn't hesitate a moment. "Yes, if that's what it
takes to ensure my children will be okay with their
lives."

"They have to live for themselves, Beth. They're not
little anymore. As a matter of fact, when the girls
came to see me last month, I hardly knew what to say
to them. They were grown women who had thoughts
and opinions that had nothing to do with me."

"And everything to do with you. They worship
you. I think they're still believing that some day you
might come to your senses and ask me to marry you."

"And would you?"

"Probably right up till last year," she admitted softly. "But then I realized just how lucky you were to find someone who was more like you. And how lucky I was to have time to grow."

They talked all through dinner. As if Beth's confession had opened a door he'd been afraid of before, Stan now felt free to talk about everything. They discussed thoughts and feelings and reflections about their lives. When dinner was over, they went into the piano bar and sat and talked some more. It was the most satisfying, deeply saddening feeling Beth had ever had.

"Closure is tough, isn't it?" Beth sighed, leaning back in the low-slung couch that sat against the wall farthest from the piano. She hadn't looked around the room, hadn't noticed it filling up. Suddenly, she felt uncomfortable, as if someone was staring at her. Watching her. Her gaze wandered over Stan's shoulder.

"Not as tough as seeing you and wondering about all the what-might-have-beens."

"Are might-have-beens the same as should-have-dones?" Duke's voice broke into their conversation; it came from behind her.

Beth turned, staring up at the man she loved. He was scowling at them unmercifully, almost as if they'd gotten caught doing something...immoral. Duke gave Stan a look that should have frozen him to the spot. "Such as 'I should have been a better husband.'

Or, 'I should have taken better care of my wife.' That kind of should-have-dones?"

Stan got up to stare at the interloper and his expression went from irritated to questioning. "Duke? Duke McGregor?"

Duke nodded.

Beth couldn't keep her eyes off him, any more than she could keep the idiotic smile off her face. He was dressed in a hand-tailored gray suit with matching shirt and red-and-black tie. His hair was wind brushed, highlighting his expensive cut. Even scowling, he looked so gorgeous—as if he'd just stepped off the pages of a menswear magazine.

Stan stuck out his hand and shook Duke's. "Haven't seen you since we last met on the golf links."

"Three years ago."

"Three years ago," Stan repeated with a genial smile. "Do you know my . . ." Stan hesitated for an instant, then recovered. "My lovely ex-wife?"

"We're neighbors," Beth interjected. Duke was still scowling, only this time his narrow-eyed gaze was fixed on her. She wondered what in heaven's name was the matter with him. Meeting under these circumstances wasn't easy, but it certainly wasn't that hard, either.

"Neighbors?" Duke asked, glaring down at her. "Is that what you call my sleeping under your roof, Beth, darling?"

"Sleeping?" Stan looked in shock as he stared at one, then the other. "You two are living together?"

"Not quite," Beth began.

"You could say that," Duke said.

Beth didn't know whose reputation she was saving, Duke's or hers, but she wasn't going to let this episode get out of hand. "Duke's bed was delivered to my condo instead of his. They haven't been able to move it yet."

"It's been there for three weeks," Duke explained. "It could have been moved at any time. You and I chose not to, that's all."

"Bed?" Stan looked in confusion from one to the other.

Duke continued to ignore Stan. His hard eyes bored into her. "Is this a new habit, or did you ever have dinner dates with other men when your husband was out of town? Or is this the way you always entertain yourself?"

"Always," Beth retorted through gritted teeth. "Don't you?"

"Only on business." Duke's tone matched hers.

"This—is—business," she hissed warningly, and then her old fear of confrontation and anger began asserting itself. She felt her stomach tighten and her nerves tense, but this time she would not give in. She would not back down from the anger. Not this time...

But Duke didn't know that. He accepted her challenge and issued one of his own. "That's funny. It doesn't look like it to me."

"What the hell's going on, here?" Stan finally demanded. "Are you two seeing each other?"

Beth stood and grabbed for her purse. "No."

Duke didn't hesitate to contradict. "Yes."

Stan glowered. "You could have told me before I made a fool of myself, Beth." She knew that tone. It meant things weren't revolving around him anymore and he was unhappy about it. For a moment, she wanted to hit *both* their heads together and knock sense into them. It was a great image.

She gave a brittle smile. "No, we aren't committed. One of us wouldn't embarrass the other if that were the case." She reached inside her purse and took out a large bill.

"Who's embarrassed?" Duke asked, cocking an angry eyebrow in her direction. "And what's the reason for embarrassment? Did someone do something wrong? If so, look to yourself."

"I already have." Chin tilted up, Beth faced him, indignation in every word. "And I've decided that you did the ugly deed." She looked from one man to the other, her disdain apparent. "Goodbye to both of you. Have a drink on me. You two have a lot in common." Duke's expression turned thunderous. She looked him square in the eye, staring him down. "Neither one of you knows me at all."

With all the grace and speed she could muster, Beth walked out of the bar and to her car. With precise movements, she drove out of the parking lot and headed toward the tall building that housed her apartment and had become her haven until now.

Anger carried her all the way home without a tear.

Despair motivated her to walk through the door.

Moments later she stood on her balcony in the dark, clutching the rail as if it were a lifeline, and wished she were a thousand miles away in a secluded garden.

Then the tears came.

9

DUKE STARED AFTER Beth's retreating figure and wondered why the hell he'd caused such a scene. Forcing his hands to unclench, he watched her trip down the stairs and disappear from the club and probably from his life. What had gotten into him that he could act that way? He'd never done anything like this before. But to do it and hurt the woman most dear to him didn't make any sense at all.

Stan interrupted his thoughts. "What the hell is going on? Why would you accuse my wife of something so terrible and make her angry?"

"I think your lovely *ex*-wife just dumped both of us," Duke stated, his mind whirling. He couldn't believe he'd embarrassed her like that and made a jackass out of himself in the bargain. A deep-down pain echoed through his limbs as he finally realized the magnitude of his actions.

"I think my lovely *ex*-wife just dumped *you*," Stan said confidently. "She'd been talking to me all evening without getting angry. So I repeat: What the hell is going on?" Stan's gaze turned hard. "Have you hurt her? Or were you just pushing her buttons? You knew she hates angry scenes so you just decided to let the relationship dive into suicide mode?"

"This is laughable." Duke brushed off his words. "You and I are standing in the middle of a bar discussing your ex-wife. Doesn't that sound a little bizarre to you?"

"It may, but we're doing it just the same," Stan stated doggedly. "Don't try to hedge your answer, Duke. What's going on here?"

Duke glared back at the man who had known Beth in a way Duke had just begun to fathom. Jealousy reared its ugly head again and Duke wanted to do something physical, like punch Stan right in his handsome face. He sorely wanted to punish him for having been with the woman he loved, but all he could do was remember that he and Stan had the same good taste. Stan had loved her, too. "It's none of your business, Stan. She's not your wife anymore, remember?" Duke caught the waitress's eye and waved for her to bring his bill. "Just stay out of it."

"We have children together. I feel responsible—" Stan stopped, then stared at Duke in awe. "My God," he finally said, the true situation finally dawning on him. "This isn't just a fling. You're in love with Beth, aren't you?"

Duke pulled out several dollar bills and threw them on top of Beth's money. He anchored it with his own beer glass. "At the risk of sounding repetitive, it's none of your business. Stay away from Beth and let her live her own life." He looked him up and down. "Have a good life, Stan. Give your new wife my sympathies."

He walked away, following Beth's path, as Stan watched in utter amazement.

Duke's footsteps seemed to echo what was becoming his favorite word: *stupid, stupid, stupid.*

He'd come back from four grueling days in Austin wanting nothing more than to be in Beth's arms. But when he was almost home, he'd remembered she had a dinner date and wouldn't be home until after ten. He'd blithely—innocently—assumed she was meeting one of her girlfriends. He hadn't wanted to face the empty apartment so he'd decided to stop off for a drink and pass the time of day with Ray, the pianist.

As the waitress had handed him his beer, he'd glanced up to see Stan and Beth looking as cozy as two old lovers—which was exactly what they were. That and more. They were perched on the couch facing each other, their expressions intent as they spoke in low tones.

He couldn't take his eyes off them, watching each respond to the other. Beth occasionally laughed or gave a smile. Stan talked intently, obviously connecting with his ex-wife in a way that made Duke see red stars. With each passing minute, his anger grew and grew until it reached such a level it boiled over. He felt himself lose his grip on his temper until at last he was so irate, he threw caution to the wind.

He'd felt jealousy before, but never to this degree. Never so much that it hurt to move a muscle.

He'd stood and walked over to join them just as Stan was declaring his desire for her to return to him—or something along those lines, he was sure.

A primitive emotion so strong it shook him to his very core had washed over him and he'd known he was going to do something stupid—he just couldn't stop.

He'd wanted to make Beth admit that she wanted Duke more than she had ever wanted her ex-husband.

He'd wanted to be the victor in front of Stan so she would never find the need to go back to her ex-husband.

Brilliant.

Instead, he'd acted like a stupid adolescent rather than a grown man who could run circles around Stan's intelligence and know-how. All he'd proved to Beth was that he could be a bigger, more stupid bore than any man she knew—*including* her ex-husband!

But, surely she could see he hadn't meant to act that way. Certainly she would know that he cared so much for her, that he— The right words failed him. All he could think of was how much he loved her. And he'd tried to turn her from the path he saw her on by lashing out at her.

He deserved an award. He'd succeeded in acting childish in front of an entire club filled with old acquaintances she hadn't even noticed were there.

Duke parked and went directly to Beth's place. He knocked, but she didn't answer. Unable to give his smile or small talk to Mrs. Rutgar's door-opening, he used his key and walked into Beth's home.

The apartment was dark, and for a moment he wondered if she was there. Her car had been parked in the garage, so she had to be around somewhere. Maybe she'd gone for a walk. He needed to find her to explain....

He turned to leave again, then noticed the open patio door.

Beth stood at the balcony rail, staring up at a laughing full moon dangling just above the trees like a ripe orange. Her hands were wrapped around the wrought-iron railing as if she was trying to stay earthbound. As if she might fly away if she let go.

He said the first words that came to mind. "God, I'm so sorry."

Her hands tightened on the rail. "So am I." Her voice was low and thick with tears.

His heart wrenched at the sound. "What are you sorry about?"

She swallowed hard and cleared her throat. "I'm sorry that we won't be seeing each other after tonight."

His heart sank to his toes. "Where am I going?"

"To your own place or wherever else you want to go. But not here. Not ever here again."

"You've still got my bed."

"You said we'd both postponed it so we could stay together. Well, then, it's time to call the movers and get it out of here. Our time together is over."

"Where will I stay until they can move it?"

She shook her head as if denying his words. "That's not my problem."

"Really?" He closed his eyes, hoping to ease the hurt and rejection he felt. "I'm sorry, I thought I was talking to the Beth who cared about me."

"You were. But that Beth doesn't ever want to be hurt and humiliated in public or in private again. The only way *that* can be assured is if you aren't around."

The truth hit him like a blow to his gut. "You *wanted* your husband back! You wanted to make up to that sorry son of a . . ."

She turned to face him, her expression cold and rigid. "Don't say another word about Stan. And don't accuse me of something you dreamed up in your own head," she warned. "You have no right. Regardless of what you think, he's the father of my children and the man I chose to live with for many years. Unless you believe my taste in men is horrible, you can't put him down. And if you *do* believe my taste in men is horrible, then where does that leave you in the grand scheme of things?"

"In love with you."

She smiled without mirth. "A jewel among men."

He didn't know what to say—how to say what he felt or how to appease her. He'd just opened up his heart and she'd stepped on it, then kicked it out the door. God! It hurt! "That's uncalled for."

"I don't think so. Right now, you look like the one I ought to be wary of. As a matter of fact, for the first time in three years, I'm recognizing a few of my ex-husband's wonderful traits that I never noticed before. It's a shame you weren't around a few years ago. You could have saved my marriage."

He didn't believe her for a moment. What a damn shame he hadn't seen it then. "Look, I admit I spoke in the heat of anger. I should have kept my mouth shut. But what I said wasn't that bad."

"You're wrong," she contradicted calmly, stubbornly. "It was, and worse because it was said in anger. You pulled accusations out of a hat, accusing us of whatever. As a matter of fact, you just did it again." Her eyes were frosty as they stared at him. "If you can get angry over my having a discussion with the father of my children, you can get angry over anything."

"That's not true."

"Your reputation precedes you, Duke. I'd heard about your temper, but until now, I'd never seen it and thought perhaps the rumors were exaggerated. Now, I know better. If you can flare over a little thing like this evening, then you might be worse over something else." Her chin tilted. "I can't live with you or claim a position in your life wondering what will make you mad enough to strike out at me, verbally or otherwise. That's not a relationship. That's a jail sentence."

He stared at her, knowing what she was saying. She wasn't so much frightened by what he'd said and done as by what she imagined he was capable of saying and doing. But his pride stung mightily at her words.

"You're shooting way ahead, aren't you? I haven't *asked* you to be in my life," he stated quietly.

If he'd slapped her in the face, he couldn't have gotten more of a reaction. By the light of the moon he saw a blush work from her neck to her forehead. "You're right. I apologize for letting my thoughts get ahead of your actions." She turned and faced the night forest once more. "If you don't mind, I'd like to have some privacy."

Duke didn't say a word. He went inside, flipped on the kitchen light and poured two glasses of wine. Then he made his way back and stepped out onto the patio. Beth didn't look at him, but she silently accepted the glass he put in her hand. He left her there and headed for his room, then undressed in the darkness and stretched out on his bed, naked.

The chilled wine felt good flowing down his throat. He wished he'd brought the whole bottle with him so he could drink it fast and deaden the vision of her chilling, angry gaze. But getting drunk wasn't the answer, damn it.

He hadn't been as angry as he'd been tonight since early in his marriage. Back then, everything had to be perfect and all had to be right. His frustration level with life was at a constant ninety-nine percent, and anything that aggravated him spilled out in anger.

No one said too much to him in those days, and so he didn't pay attention to the fact that he spouted off more than the average guy. He just figured the average guy wasn't smart or quick or right enough to fight for what he thought was right. Then one night, Duke had seen the intense fear in his son's eyes when he'd gone on a rampage about toys in the driveway.

For a brief, zinging moment, he'd seen himself as others had, and he'd marveled at how he could have thought himself smart and right. He'd been neither. He'd been a blustering, stupid fool.

The very next week, he'd signed up for a class on controlling anger. It wasn't easy learning all the different alternative responses. But within a year, he'd finally learned how to control himself and what it took for him to do so. He'd also learned that no one ever got anything by instilling fear—not for long, anyway. And all these years since, he'd been careful to realize and recognize the danger signals and make sure that he never put himself in that place again.

Yet, although he'd never thought he would repeat that mistake, he was once more in that position.

A saying he'd kept in his mind like a banner in those early days came back to him now. *You will not be punished FOR your anger, you will be punished BY your anger.* Its truth rang out again, just as it had several years ago.

He had tried to punish the woman he loved, and he'd punished himself.

He would leave early tomorrow morning. . . .

BETH WALKED THROUGH the days that followed like a zombie. Her thoughts were never far from the scene in the piano bar. Her mind was always able to review the memory of Duke's face as he stared down at her and Stan. It was frightening. He'd been so angry, but the anger itself hadn't been as frightening as knowing what he might be capable of.

Oh, the scene hadn't been so very bad. It was the knowing that if they ever had an argument and he lost his temper, she wouldn't feel safe.

She railed against the fates. She railed against chance. She railed against her love for Duke. She even railed against herself.

Growing up, she'd never told anyone about her father's anger. Around the time she married Stan and began a family, her father died of a heart attack—a well-deserved one. He'd always been upset about something or someone. He'd always been unhappy about whatever—the newspaper wasn't delivered on the front step just right, the man at the fast-food restaurant didn't give him everything in his order, or the kid in the grocery store spoke with an accent that he couldn't understand. It didn't matter to him that the paper was thrown from a truck at three in the morning, that the man in the fast-food restaurant didn't know that crackers or syrup were supposed to accompany the order, or that her father couldn't speak *one* language correctly, let alone the two the young kid in the grocery store spoke.

Nothing suited him. Nothing. He was the most unhappy man in the world. It took Beth until adulthood to realize that anything that detracted from his wife's complete attention to him was another problem—including his daughter. He forgot that Beth was his flesh and blood, too. She was just a child and demanded her mother's time, and that meant she and her father were in competition.

She'd never told Duke about her fear of a temper. She'd never thought she needed to. But now, she realized she should have. It was an important factor in her life and she'd never mentioned it—perhaps because she felt that discussing it would be inviting problems. If it wasn't spoken about, then it wasn't real.

Beth had had a more-than-unhappy childhood. It had been miserable. She used to think that her house was the only one where it rained on the inside while the sun shone outside.

After her marriage, the residue of her father's attitude still clung to her. Stan changed that. Slowly and with patience, he showed her that, although most men have tempers, not all men have *violent* tempers. He'd explained that most people learned to control themselves as they grew up. After a while, she also realized that she had to change her attitude to a happier one or she would bring her own father's sour attitude into her children's upbringing. That, she would not allow.

Now, years later, she'd flashed back to that part of her life she wished she could forget the most—the part she refused to ever, *ever* return to.

And it was all tied up with the man she loved.

Every fifteen minutes she would begin crying, then sniffle, then work some more. It was a cycle—one she couldn't seem to break.

Although Beth was awake, Duke had left her house early the next morning without speaking a word in her direction. He knew, just as she did, that it was over.

Beth blamed herself for getting so involved with Duke before she'd found out more about him.

Stupid.

Not her. Not him. The circumstances. If she'd been anyone else, she could probably cope with that side of him. They would have had one hell of an argument, but it would have been over. But she was her father's daughter and there was no changing that. His anger was imprinted on her.

It took time to dredge up old lessons and remember that she shouldn't have to *cope* with his temper. There was no excuse for Duke's behavior and she didn't deserve his comments under any circumstances.

The best thing that could happen was that someone would call and make arrangements to get his bed out of her home.

Three nights later, Beth got the call she'd been expecting.

"Is this Beth McGruder?" a female voice questioned.

Her heart sank to her feet. "Yes, it is."

"This is Judy. I'm a friend of Duke's?" The woman's Texas drawl ended each sentence with a question. "And I'm calling to make sure that everything is set up for the bed to be moved tomorrow?"

"Tomorrow? That's Tuesday. I'm afraid I can't be here to see it out the door."

"That's okay. I understand that your condo management company will be more than happy to let them in as long as you okay it ahead of time?"

Beth took a deep breath. She had no right to hold his bed at the same time she was kicking him out of it. "Fine. I'll give it to them tonight."

"Oh, thank you," Judy said sweetly, and Beth felt as if she was being patronized, but she couldn't prove it. "You're so very kind. Duke told me you've really been nice to him and how much he appreciated it. You've gone out of your way to be accommodating."

The disappointment turned into a slow-burning anger. "Did he really?"

"Oh, yes. He mentioned how thoughtful you've been. Why, he even said that he felt sorry for taking advantage of you the way he has?" Judy laughed. "But you know how men are?"

"I'm beginning to," Beth stated between clenched teeth.

"Well, I'll talk to you later. Thanks again?" Judy hung up.

Beth tried all night long to hold down her temper, but anger seethed just below the surface. Men! They were so cocky and sure of themselves! Duke included! Duke *especially!*

Who did he think he was to have his girlfriend call to make arrangements to move his bed! What callousness could invade his very spirit so that he would not only be mean, but figuratively slap her in the face with another woman! Where was his sense of decency?

And one more question kept pecking at her. *Where was his remorse for his behavior at the piano bar?*

After her anger, came sadness; the deep, heavy-inside kind that hurt so much she didn't want to move—not even across the room.

And by late night, Beth could no longer contain the unstoppable supply of tears. She cried until she thought she would die from the heartbreak.

It wasn't until almost morning that she faced the fact that her love for Duke was deeper, broader, more complete than for anyone she'd ever known.

And because of his temper, she'd lost him.

She would carry that loss with her for the rest of her life.

Damn Duke McGregor for ruining her chance at happiness!

Damn Duke McGregor!

DUKE'S CELL PHONE rang hollowly in the sterile hotel room, and he reached over to turn down the football game on TV before picking it up and turning it on.

"Hey, Dad. How are things?" Benji's upbeat voice momentarily raised Duke's spirits.

"Hey, fine. What's up, son?"

"Well, I just had to call and let you know what happened last weekend. I knew you'd get a jolt out of it."

"Jolt me. I could use it," Duke stated dryly.

"I went to Austin and guess who I ran into at one of the dances?"

Duke couldn't think of a thing. He didn't want to play games. Not now. "Who?"

"The McGruder twins!" Benji laughed. "Isn't that something? You talk about them and I run into them! Scary, huh?"

"Not so scary since that's where they go to school."

"Yeah, well. Anyway. I danced with the more outgoing one. You know—Cassandra?"

"I've met her," Duke said slowly, wondering where his son was going with this.

"Well, I asked her how her mom was doing and all that, ya know?"

"Go on."

"And they asked me about your temper and how mean you were and said you sure didn't look it when they met you."

Duke remembered the incident. He'd been more interested in Beth than her daughters but he did remember they were very beautiful—almost as beautiful as their mother.

"Anyway, I told them I hadn't seen you angry since I was seven years old and left my bike in the driveway after you'd been traveling for a week or two. I told them you'd handled that pretty good. In fact, you went through the divorce without ever losing your temper with Mom."

Benji was right. Until the evening in the bar, he'd been sure that he didn't have a temper anymore. That incident had taught him just how wrong he'd been.

"And then I asked about their witch of a mother who used to look out for them as if they were always ready to do something horrible. I told them it was obvious that their mother never trusted them. And you know what they said?"

"I wonder." Duke knew the answer, but he was going to go through the motions anyway. This was his son's conversation and it was important to hear him out.

"They said that their mom wasn't a witch, she was just protective. And they're still close to her." Benji took a breath. "Isn't that a riot? All this time I thought she was a witch, and she was, but it was kinda, like, she was a good witch, you know?"

"I know." Duke's voice was low. Images of Beth filled his mind night and day. He loved her more than . . . "She's a special lady."

"Well," Benji began awkwardly. "I just wanted you to know that I, uh, well, if you wanted to date her, I guess I can't complain too much. You're smart enough to know what you're getting into."

Duke had to smile. "Good thought. Especially since I've been around for double the years you have. I must have learned something by this time."

"Well—" his son laughed "—things have changed a lot since your day, Dad. There're some women out there who'd love to get a hold of you for your money. You know what I mean?"

"I'll keep that in mind, son. The next time there's a lesson to be learned, I'll call and check it out with you."

"Good thought. Can't be too careful," Benji advised, but there was a tinge of humor in his voice. "And while you're at it, Dad, why don't you ask Mrs. McGruder to help you pick out some great leather furniture? Something that looks better than what you've got."

"You don't like my stuff?"

"No," Benji replied without taking even a second to think about it. "Mrs. McGruder could warm it up a little, maybe. A woman's touch, you know? She could mix your idea of leather with her own stuff and make it look, uh, better."

Duke wished.

He thought of Beth finally seeing his apartment, and knew his lack of style would awe and amaze her. He had never allowed her inside, knowing she would think his taste was in his feet, which, according to what he saw every time he walked in, was true. But he'd needed furniture in a hurry and had bought a set that looked good on the showroom floor.

He'd planned to show Beth sometime and they could both have a laugh over it. Then she would tell him it didn't matter and he could toss it out. Together, they would find something that suited them both. Something in real Italian leather that would mesh with her furniture and his masculine tastes . . .

He and Benji talked for another five or ten minutes about all the things going on in his son's life and that of his friends. But no matter where the conversation went, it always came back to girls again. It made Duke realize just how much his own child had grown up.

"Remember, son. It's not necessary to marry until you're out of college and established. In fact, the longer you wait, the better it might be."

"I know, Dad. I'm not going to rush into anything. I've got the rest of my life to find that kind of happiness. Believe me, after watching you and Mom, I'm not jumping off the deep end so I can suffer more later on. I saw that already."

"Sorry you had to learn that lesson from us, Ben. I would have done it better if I could."

Divorce was a hell of a way of teaching youth to do better. He only hoped his son would find the happiness Duke had just lost. One of them should be lucky.

When he hung up the phone, Duke realized that his son had just given him his blessing to have a relationship with the woman he loved. It would have been funny if it hadn't been so sad. All along, Benjamin had said no to his relationship. Now that Beth wasn't in his life anymore, his son had given his okay.

And it was too late.

Damn him for losing his cool.

He wished Beth missed him half as much as he missed her.

10

BETH SPRAWLED in the center of her bed in the dark, the phone clasped to her ear. Her daughters were taking turns telling a very long story about meeting Benji at a sorority dance. Beth didn't want to hear it, but she was a captive audience. Every word they said about the young man brought the image of his father back to her memory in living color. Life was tough enough, yet here she was, torturing herself with thoughts of Duke.

Even her wonderful fantasy bed wasn't the same. It needed Duke....

"And so, when we were through discussing you, we discussed Mr. McGregor. Do you know what he said, Mom?" Cassandra asked.

Beth was startled back to the present. "Wait a minute, wait a minute. Back up. What did you say about discussing me?"

"Mo-om. Didn't you hear us? Benji said that he remembered you were like a witch, never letting us go to the park alone. And we weren't allowed to go to gymnastics without you sitting there—sitting anywhere we went. You didn't just drop us off, you stayed."

She was missing some of the conversation and tried to quickly catch up. "And that was wrong?"

"Well," her daughter said, struggling to find words her mother would accept. "He thought you might have been . . . a little overprotective. We told him you were. And that you were the brightest, sweetest, funniest mom anyone could ever have."

"Thank you. I think." Her voice was dry, but she warmed at the compliment. Most of the time the girls hardly said a word about her doing a good job of being their mom, so praise was a rarity and something to treasure.

"You're welcome. And then we asked him about his dad. You know, he used to say his dad had the worst temper of anyone he'd ever seen."

"I suppose." All Beth's attention was focused on her daughter's words now.

"And he said that when he was a kid, his father's temper was known far and wide. No one ever said anything to him because they were afraid of being yelled at, so they just ignored him or stayed out of his way. But Mr. McGregor was under such stress he didn't notice it himself. And then one day he realized just how strong his temper was and he quit. Benji said he was seven at the time but that he remembers it as if it was yesterday."

"He quit? Just like that?"

"Just like that," Carol said. "But what Cassandra forgot to mention is that Mr. McGregor went into therapy to make sure it wouldn't happen again. And he didn't play mind games in there, he honestly wanted to lick the problem. Apparently it worked, because Benji says he hasn't seen his father lose his temper *once* in *all those years!* Benji says that his dad discussed this with him several times, because he didn't want his son to be scarred or have a temper he thought he couldn't control when in, fact, everyone could control themselves."

All those years. Benji was almost twenty. And as Beth had seen, Duke's temper was just below the surface.

"Well, I'm glad for Benji. I know it's not fun being around someone with a temper. At least Duke tried to shield his son from that."

"I said, 'Is that why your mom used to threaten you with his temper?' and he said, 'Mum never forgave him for the years before.' Isn't that something? Benji's mom perpetuated that."

Beth thought of all the times her father had gotten in her mother's face and yelled and screamed. "It might be that what he hid from his son, his wife wasn't able to escape."

"No, Mom, I don't think so. Benji was pretty sure his dad hadn't blown his fuse in forever."

She didn't believe that. She couldn't—it would mean that she'd just thrown away the most wonderful relationship she'd ever had for nothing. "Well, I'm glad you two got along with Benji."

"Got along?" Cassandra laughed. "God, he's *adorable*, Mom! He's changed so much since we were in school. He's really so very adult and *knowledge-able.*"

"*Benji?*"

"Ben, Mom. Benji is a kid's name. Or a dog's. This is a definite guy." She drawled out the last two words. "And he's so neat, I hope he comes back to school soon."

"Wasn't he with somebody?" Beth asked, trying to stay focused on the conversation at hand. "I thought he had a date with some girl."

"Oh, he didn't even know her very well. He was just doing it as a favor to her brother, who's a fraternity brother of his. He's not dating anyone right now."

"How do you know?"

"Because I asked!" Cassandra made it sound like the most natural thing in the world. Her daughter had come into her own. She knew what she wanted and asked for it. When Beth was her age, she would never have said a word.

"Times have certainly changed," she mused.

"So, how is Mr. McGregor?" Cassandra sounded coy, as if she already knew the answer.

"I'm sure he's fine, honey. I haven't seen him lately."

"You haven't? How come?"

"Because his bed was moved last week, and he doesn't stay here anymore."

"Damn—darn! Sorry, Mom."

Beth ignored the curse. She felt like cursing, herself. "It was his bed, honey."

"I know, but—"

"And you weren't too fond of him being here the last time I spoke to you."

"I was wrong," her daughter said quickly. "I thought he was shallow and that he had a temper."

There was a silence Beth couldn't fill. She didn't know what to say.

Carol interjected, "She means, well, you know how tempers were in our family, Mom. We don't need someone else like Grandpa around."

"You don't remember Grandpa, honey."

"No, but I remember hearing that you and Grandma were afraid of him when you were growing up. Sometimes Dad was afraid to raise his voice because of the way you'd react."

"And so he should. You don't have to raise your voice to make a point."

"You don't have to run away, either," Carol stated quietly.

Her daughter's soft words hammered Beth over the head with their wisdom. She thought of all kinds of wonderful, witty things to say, but truth and honesty won the day. She'd learned a lot in the past two years, and denying it now would be a shame. "I wish I could say something else, honey. But you're right. I'm not running away anymore if I can help it."

"Does that mean you'll consider dating Mr. McGregor?"

"I appreciate your blessing," she replied, deliberately attempting to keep her tone light. "But Mr. McGregor hasn't asked me out. In fact, I believe he has a girlfriend, already. His bed was moved to her home."

"Are you telling me—" Cassandra's voice sounded high-pitched and disbelieving "—that some woman has such bad taste that she *asked* for that bed to be in her *home?*"

Judy's sugar-sweet voice echoed in Beth's ear and she suddenly felt worn-out. Emotionally, her spirits had gone through the wringer, and her daughter was making sure she was drained. "That's right. And although I appreciate your caring, honey, I'd rather not talk about it."

"Okay, Mom," Cassandra said reluctantly, for once not arguing. Quickly, Carol changed the subject to school. The subject of Duke McGregor was dropped.

When Beth hung up the phone, she crawled under the down comforter and, holding a pillow to her stomach, she curled into a ball. Within minutes, she was crying. The pain of losing Duke was almost too much to bear, and she had no other way to let out the sadness.

An hour later, she fell asleep. Dreams of a wonderful life with Duke were tainted by his anger in every circumstance she envisioned. But it was the last one that woke her up to stare unseeingly through the dark at the ceiling. She had had enough and had told him so. He listened with love in his eyes, and finally kissed her—long and slow and sweet.

Beth woke up. Her heart beat so rapidly in her chest, it took several minutes for her to regain her calm. She wanted Duke, but she was fantasizing if she thought she could change him. No one could change or rearrange someone else, no matter how hard they tried. Why, she wondered, couldn't life be like she wanted it to be?

She laughed aloud at that naive question, because it was laughable. Life was nothing if not a compromise. She could either accept Duke McGregor with a temper or not accept him at all.

At the thought of acceptance, her heart raced, her throat closed up and her ears rang with fear.

Although she'd never loved a man so much or so well, her gut reaction made the choice simple.

DUKE DROVE AROUND with the real-estate agent all day long. He'd decided it was time to use a little of the money he'd set aside and do what he wanted to do: buy a house. It had to have lots of trees and privacy and still be close to stores and shops.

Was it too much to ask for a perfect house? There hadn't been one that came close to his expectations in the twenty or more he'd seen so far.

The weary agent dropped him off at the condo after seven o'clock and disappeared before Duke was inside. Instead of heading toward his own place, he went to Beth's door.

He knocked several times, rousing only Mrs. Rutgar. She peeped from the security of her door and he waved. "Hi, Mrs. Rutgar. I'm looking for Beth. Know where she is?"

"On a date," she said. The chain was off the door, but her usual smile was gone. He was obviously not in good favor anymore. He missed her approval.

Duke's heart pounded hard against his chest. Then he asked the most stupid question of all. "With a man?"

"Of course," the little woman replied. Then, as if sensing an upcoming explosion, she quickly shut the door and flipped the lock.

He took a deep breath and, with measured steps, walked down the hall. As the elevator took him upstairs, he closed his eyes and promised himself he was in control.

Once upstairs, he went to the refrigerator and grabbed a beer. It took a minute for him to realize what he was doing and he put the unopened brew back on the shelf, then dressed for exercise. It was time to take a run.

Later that night, he stood on his balcony and stared at the same silhouette of pines he'd seen so often from Beth's balcony just one floor below.

He'd had it made. He'd found heaven and hadn't known it until the night he'd lost it.

Beth. Beth was his heaven, his paradise.

If someone had told him how much love hurt just a few months ago, he would have laughed at them. He never would have believed it. But now, he ached as he had never ached before.

He had to do something to make her see how wrong she was not to let him back into her life. He just didn't know what.

BETH STRETCHED OUT on the couch and tried to read her newest pop-psychology book. Some writer had decided that more than one man really wanted to figure out how to think like a woman, understand like a woman and have the same in-depth relationships women were looking for.

Baloney. It was the only word Beth could think of to describe the book. If men were as mindless as this writer made them out to be, then why were women wanting them in their lives to begin with?

She'd had a blind date the other night and it was the most boring evening she'd ever spent. Kay and Gene had set her up with a friend, though, and she'd figured it was time to taste life a little. She'd been burying herself lately.

Her date's name was Arnie and they went to dinner and a movie. The movie was an action adventure. Whoever wrote it hadn't spent more than an hour on the script. It contained maybe three pages of dialogue and at least twenty killings. Beth hadn't known there were that many ways to get blown away.

Dinner was cheap—Mexican food that tasted like cardboard, only with five times the calories of regular food. Her date scoffed it down as if it was his last meal—then ate her leftovers. The conversation was stilted and boring, neither one really being interested in the other.

Beth had finally decided that life was too short to spend it with people she didn't know and didn't *want* to know.

She would spent the rest of her life at home thumbing through magazines before she would date another Arnie.

But when someone knocked on the door, she was grateful for the possibility of company.

A shock of pleasure seared through her body when she saw Duke's handsome face. He was leaning against her doorjamb in faded jeans and a blue denim shirt, looking sexier than any man had a right to look. He smiled as his gaze intimately drifted down her T-shirt-clad chest, then back up again. "I know you won't believe this, but I need a hug. Real bad."

A wave of intense longing swept over her and she had to hold her breath to keep from drowning. She fought to keep her distance and resist throwing herself in his arms. "Well, you poor thing," she murmured sweetly. "I hope you find one."

She started to shut the door. Her heart was racing so hard, she could barely catch her breath. Damn him! *Damn him!*

He reached out, stopping the door. "Wait. Please." His voice changed from teasing to pleading. "I need to talk to you."

"It doesn't work when it's a one-way street, Duke. I don't need to talk to you. Your bed is gone to your new girlfriend's house and there's nothing more to say."

"My bed has gone where the company was ordered to move it. Judy didn't ask me if I wanted the bed moved, she just took it upon herself to get it done. She knew how I felt about you and thought her little ploy might work. She was wrong."

Beth felt a perverse sense of satisfaction, knowing that Judy had goofed and Duke hadn't really wanted to leave. But it didn't change anything, not really.

When she didn't answer, he continued, "She knew better than to have it set up in her place, though. It's in my apartment."

"So now the wrong bed is in the right place."

"There was nothing wrong about that bed. It brought us together. And I'm damn glad it did."

"I'm happy for you," she said, using anything, including sarcasm, to keep her distance from a man who was so obviously not good for her.

"Please, Beth. Talk to me."

"We've already said everything there is to say."

"No, *you* said everything," Duke argued. "I never had a chance to explain or to tell you what my remedy was."

"I don't need to know. It's none of my business."

"I want it to be your business."

Her insides churned, her muscles tensed. She had to remain distant. She had to protect herself. She wondered frantically what had happened to her inbred survival instinct. It wasn't paying a bit of attention or giving her any help. "It doesn't matter what you want. It matters what *I* want. Your temper won't fit in my life. I won't allow it. Ever."

"You're a hard lady," he began, but she was in motion to close the door. He stopped it once more. "Wait!" At her hesitation, he began speaking fast. "I know I did wrong. I know it more than you'll ever know. Because of one slip I may well lose the woman I love. But whether I do or I don't, I need to apologize to you and tell you I recognize just how wrong I was."

The door across the hall opened and Mrs. Rutgar peered out the crack, one inquisitive eye watching them.

Duke turned his charm on her. "Hello, Mrs. Rutgar. I'm apologizing to Beth, but she won't listen. I'm hoping I can talk her into giving me just one more chance."

"Beth knows what she's doing," Mrs. Rutgar said with finality; but her door remained ajar.

Duke looked at Beth, his blue eyes seeing more than she wanted him to. "I get the feeling you're angry about something that has nothing to do with me. You've got some baggage you're carrying around."

Those words brought her survival instinct to life. "Don't you *dare* brush your actions off on me." Her voice was low and tight, her eyes spewing fire at him. "That puts the problem on my shoulders, and I don't deserve that. I won't accept it."

"You're angry?" Duke asked, astonishment in his tone. "I've never heard you shout."

"I'm furious," she replied, her hands clenched at her sides. "When you decided you didn't have to control yourself, you took away my dreams for our future. I had my own secret thoughts and wishes and wants about us, and your actions destroyed them. You never gave a thought to my needs that night. Only to your own. I'm so angry with you for trampling on that!"

He hung his head. "God, I know. I know, and I'm sorry."

Beth wasn't to be appeased. "Well, buddy, sorry isn't good enough."

"Give me one more chance, Beth. Please." He reached out to touch her, but the look in her eyes told him not to try. His hand dropped to his side.

He was wreaking havoc with her emotions. Part of her wanted to burrow into his chest and tell the world to go to hell in a handbasket. But her fear overcame both his pleas and her weakness.

The cold, disconnected look in his eyes when he had lashed out at her that night was enough to remind her of worse times. She never wanted to be the focus of such rage again. Which meant she could never be around him again. The decision had been made.

"No." Her voice was dead, devoid of all emotion. She refused to let herself feel anything. Once she'd closed the door on Duke and she had her privacy, she would cry her eyes out. But not now, not when he and Mrs. Rutgar were watching.

Duke's expression mirrored the sadness she felt. "That was the first time I ever slipped like that. All I can say in my defense is that I was never so scared. I'd just found you and admitted to myself that I loved you more than I'd ever loved a woman before, and suddenly I thought that I was going to lose you to a man who'd already had his chance and lost it." His gaze seared her. "Stan hadn't treated you right for years, Beth. We both know that. Yet, there you were, talking to him as if he'd just hung the moon again."

She shook her head in denial. "It doesn't matter. Even if I had decided to be with Stan, it was my choice. You had no right to lash out at me. You aren't a child who has to learn how to behave to be part of the human race. You're a *grown man!*"

"I know," he admitted. "I was just as shocked as you were. I've gone back into counseling."

"Good." Her voice was laced with both anger and satisfaction. "And while you're at it, talk about all the other women in your life. Talk about being unable to make a commitment to one while you're dating a bunch of others."

"Please." Duke reached out and stroked her shoulder, her arm. His fingers were soothing and electrifying at the same time. "There's no one else for me but you. I swear. Judy's gone. And I love you. Just you."

"It doesn't matter. I can't trust you."

Duke looked over his shoulder. "What do you think, Mrs. Rutgar? Do you think I'm worth one more try?"

"Don't know," the widow began. "Beth's the only one who can make that decision. She has to be right with whatever decision she makes. It's her life."

Duke turned back to Beth. "I've done all the apologizing I can do. It's up to you now." He took one step closer. They weren't touching but if she'd raised her finger, she could have stroked his cheek. The temptation was so great....

"I love you," he said.

Unable to speak, Beth shook her head, took a step back and closed the door slowly but firmly. Three little words. He'd used the right three little words, but he hadn't used them until he was in a pinch. What with everything that came before, they didn't ring true. The latch clicked securely and Beth leaned against the door, eyes closed. No tears came, there was no lump in her throat. Nothing.

Instead, blessed, blessed numbness seeped into her bones from head to toe. She could have been run over by an eighteen-wheeler, and she wouldn't have felt a thing.

Like a mechanical doll, she went through the motions of emptying the dishwasher and tidying up the kitchen. Then, turning out all the lights as she went, she walked out to the patio and sat down on the chaise longue with a large glass of wine. The breeze was light and little puffs of cloud skimmed across the dark sky. She stared at nothing, felt nothing.

But the numbness didn't last forever. As the minutes became an hour, "nothing" became heartrending pain. A low moan gathered in her breast, but she refused to let it out. She would not allow it a voice and make it real. No. This wasn't the end of the world. The pain of love healed.

The brave talk worked for a while, but then another bout of tears would hit. She would want to cry and moan, but once more she would go through the pep talk.

Suddenly, she raised her head and sniffed. The cool night air carried the aroma of Duke's favorite cigar. For a moment she thought it was wishful thinking, a remembrance of those evenings when he'd finished dinner with a cigar on the patio. Then she realized the smoke was drifting down from his patio, swirling on a strange current of air.

Her breath caught in her throat and she was almost afraid to move for fear he would know she was right below him. He might feel the anguish in her heart, interpret her movements in his mind; read her thoughts and hold her soul for ransom. He might absorb her back into him—and then she would be lost.

The price was too dear.

Very quietly, she stood and turned toward the doors to her bedroom. But then she heard Duke's low voice. "Star light, star bright, I wish the wish I wish tonight. Please, let Beth remember that one great love lasts a lifetime."

With tears in her eyes, Beth went into her bedroom and slowly but firmly shut the door behind her. Then she lay down on her fantasy bed and remembered the better-than-good, loving times she and Duke had shared in this very bed. She wished she knew what in heaven's name she was doing. And whatever it was, she hoped it was right.

DUKE HEARD THE SCREEN door close and knew Beth had been on her patio. He'd thought so, but hadn't been sure. Every instinct urged him to run downstairs, take her into his arms and never let her go. He'd promised the full moon that he would never hurt her again. He'd done everything he could. Now, if their love was worth anything, he wanted her to admit how much she loved him. He wanted her to stop hurting them both, and yet, he didn't know how to make that happen.

There had to be a way. There had to be....

ON THURSDAY, Beth got home at the usual time. She kicked off her shoes, stripped down and slipped into a long T-shirt. Just as she was making up her mind between two different TV dinners, the doorbell rang.

A young man stood there holding the largest bouquet she'd ever seen. "For you, ma'am."

Beth stared in wonder. "Are those lilacs?"

"Yes, ma'am. Two dozen. And two dozen yellow daisies."

He brought the flowers inside and she found him a tip. Alone again, she sat on the couch and stared at the bouquet.

The spray was so large it could stand in a corner and be a major part of the decor. Or it could act as a privacy screen for the sliding-glass doors out to the patio.

Beth started laughing. It had to be Duke. He'd never heard of a dozen red roses. Oh, no. He'd had to go for the "grand gesture."

Just when she was getting used to not having him in her life. Just when she was getting used to being alone again.

For the first time she noticed the envelope tucked into the back of the large brass pot. It took every ounce of nerve she had to open it. She assumed it was from Duke and that it would be written persuasively, guaranteed to touch her heart and wilt all her stoic cynicism.

She was right all the way around.

Dear Beth,

I recognize that only you can make the decision to allow me in your life. I might have lost my temper once, but it was once in a very long time. However, would you consider that your reaction to me might be because you're more afraid of me and our love than of my anger? I wish you luck and love and lots of other great feelings. And maybe, just a little rain so you remember how wonderful sunshine is.

I love you.

The tears came then. They gushed and ran in rivers down her face as if they would never stop. She hurt everywhere. She craved Duke's arms, his smile, his thoughts, his caring.

Stop it, her mind screamed. *Just stop it!*

She'd fallen in love and lost once before. It had taken her years of knowing and not admitting that the marriage was over when it really was. And then years after knowing the marriage was over, to admit that it was a failure.

Now, history was repeating itself. This had to stop. Now.

FRIDAY EVENING she arrived home to find a giant framed photo of a rambling two-story home with a Sold sign on the lawn. It was the kind of home that looked as if the owners never wanted to leave. Written on the photo by the curb mailbox in black pen were the names: Mr. Duke McGregor, and just below, Ms. Beth McGruder. And below that: And Families.

The well-tended gardens and flower beds around the trees and house were beautiful and in full bloom. Her hands itched to till the soil. Her heart ached with the beauty of it.

Attached was a note. She opened it slowly, her hands trembling as she did so.

What about giving me a six-month trial period to prove to you just how much I love you? I'm like a revolving account—you can always return the merchandise. Let's be happy together, darling. If you don't accept this offer, I'm doomed to wander the inside of this empty house alone— and pick all the wrong furniture.

I love you.

Beth let herself into the apartment and set the picture on the coffee table. She stared hard at the photo and thought of the note clamped firmly in her hand. It was time to stop crying and mourning and truly decide what was real. Right now.

No one was given a guarantee that things would be perfect for them down the road. She could either choose to be alone or find out if she could share the rest of her life with Duke. She was a big girl now, and her daddy wasn't there to yell at her until she cowered in a corner. She could at least fight like a grown woman instead of reacting like a child.

Duke's idea was a good one. A trial period would give them both a chance to see if they could live and be together.

What it came down to was that she could take a chance and grab at this happiness, or she could run scared for the rest of her life.

She was quick to make up her mind. But it took forever for her to reach for the phone and dial his number.

When he answered, she spoke.

"One year instead of six months." Her tone was firm and uncompromising.

"I don't agree, but we can negotiate."

"No pushing for a wedding date until the year is over."

"Maybe."

"You're sure about this?" she finally asked, her own fears still cooking on the back burner. "You really love me?"

His voice when he replied was strong and sure. "I've never been more sure in my life. I really truly love you, my Beth. I apologize for striking out at you the other night, but I won't continue to apologize for the rest of my life. I made a mistake. It won't happen again. And at the end of all this, Ms. McGruder, you owe me a wedding."

"One year, and I agree." For the first time since he'd left on that fateful trip to Austin, Beth was completely happy.

"In that case, you'd better come up here to discuss terms. I have a boatload of plans to talk to you about."

"I . . ." she began.

"No excuses. It's a fifty-fifty share, darling. You need to come up here. Besides, I want you to see just how nicely my bed fits in this apartment. You've never seen it here."

She remembered just how ugly that bed was. "Uh, Duke, about your bed."

"That's not negotiable, darling." His voice was firm. "I know it's a horror, according to decorators, but it's all mine. Come on up and help me initiate it."

Beth practically ran out the door. As she was flipping the lock, Mrs. Rutgar opened the door and stuck her head all the way out. Beth hadn't seen her do that since she'd moved in.

"Well, what do you think? Is he worth it?" the old woman demanded, with a glint of humor in her eyes.

"I think so. I'm discussing terms with him now." Beth laughed.

"Good." Mrs. Rutgar nodded her gray head, making her topknot bob. "Love is rare, my dear, and as precious as life. Remind him to treat it that way." Her eyes twinkled. "And always make sure he feels like he's given just a little more than you have. It'll keep him on his toes."

"Wonderful advice." Beth laughed again, her heart as buoyant as love could make it.

"Good. And you can wear my wedding dress. It will look as if it was made for you."

"Your wedding dress?" Beth asked, surprised. "You still have it?"

"It's a Fortuni," the old woman stated proudly. "It brings wonderful luck to the wearer and tames the savage beast." She nodded sagely. "And, my dear, I like your young man. He's a bit of a rogue—I can see the devilment in his eyes. Never a dull moment with that one. That means you'll be happy the rest of your life. I'm sure of it."

"I wish I were that sure," Beth murmured.

"Have faith. That's all you're missing. Believe me, I know these things. I've been storing up wisdom for all these years. He's already made his big mistake, so he'll be on his toes not to make another one soon. My advice to you, my dear, is to commit to 'forever' and reach for heaven. It's right there, within your grasp."

And Beth believed her.

TWO MONTHS LATER, she made a decision. Never had she known such happiness as she felt living with Duke. They became more blended with each day that passed. Her unfounded fears were gone and in their place was such an overwhelming feeling of love that she sometimes broke into a sweat just thinking about how close she'd come to losing him. Had he not confronted her, pestered her into living with him, she might never have seen him again. And if she had missed this . . .

Walking out to the patio, she sat on the edge of the lounge chair where Duke lay catnapping in the early afternoon. Tall pines provided shade, while the sun poured onto the lush, green golf-course fairway farther out. "Duke?"

Eyes closed, he reached out and pulled her head down to his chest to kiss the top of her head. "Hmm?"

"Do you really love me?" she asked.

"Very much," he murmured, his eyes sill closed. "For always and ever."

"Forever and ever?"

He smiled sleepily. "Yes."

"And will you be true? Never look at another woman?"

"Never," he promised. "Unless Cher decides she wants a boy toy. Then I reserve the right to rethink the situation. Since that isn't likely to happen, it's safe to say you've got me forever."

She gave a sigh and kissed the hollow of his throat. "Okay, big boy. Since Cher hasn't called, you can have me."

Her words took a minute to sink in. Duke's eyes popped open. He searched her face as if to reassure himself that he'd heard correctly. "I can?"

Beth nodded, her smile growing. "I want a small wedding—no more than forty or fifty people. I want champagne and lots of food. We'll write the ceremony ourselves and explain to our friends how the wrong beds turned out to be the right beds—for us, I mean." She planted a kiss on his mouth. "And I want Mrs. Rutgar to be our special guest, because she's known us from the beginning. And we'll have an all-afternoon celebration so everyone has a great time and goes home and says, 'Isn't that couple just a *hoot?*' and laughs to themselves."

"Are you serious?"

"Yes," she answered, giving him another kiss. "Except that no matter what, your bed will never be right. It's ugly and I'm glad it's in the guest bedroom, where the kids can enjoy its, uh, unusual qualities."

"I mean about the wedding," Duke clarified. "You're ready now?"

"Yes. How about you? Are you still willing?"

Duke chuckled. "Don't pass Go and don't collect two hundred dollars. We're heading for the chapel now. I can't wait to make an honest woman out of you."

"But the wedding..."

"We'll be married again in a month with all the pomp and circumstance and joy you want. Hell, you can rent an entire circus to entertain the guests. But I want you to say 'I do' in front of a justice of the peace right now, before you change your mind."

"I do," she whispered in his ear. "If you do."

And they did....

Epilogue

THREE MONTHS LATER, the following announcement appeared in the local paper.

Duke McGregor and Beth McGruder were married Friday afternoon in the beautiful azalea garden at their home on Champions Golf Course. Some sixty guests attended, including their children, Cassandra and Carol McGruder and Benjamin McGregor, all graduates of our local high school. In an unusual ceremony, the bride, wearing an ivory and ice blue Fortuni original, was given away by Mrs. Leona Rutgar. The newlyweds will spend three weeks in Italy, where they plan to shop for leather furniture.

MILLION DOLLAR SWEEPSTAKES

SWP-M96

UNLOCK THE DOOR TO GREAT ROMANCE AT BRIDE'S BAY RESORT

Join Harlequin's new across-the-lines series, set in an exclusive hotel on an island off the coast of South Carolina.

Seven of your favorite authors will bring you exciting stories about fascinating heroes and heroines discovering love at Bride's Bay Resort.

Look for these fabulous stories coming to a store near you beginning in January 1996.

Harlequin American Romance #613 in January
Matchmaking Baby by Cathy Gillen Thacker

Harlequin Presents #1794 in February
Indiscretions by Robyn Donald

Harlequin Intrigue #362 in March
Love and Lies by Dawn Stewardson

Harlequin Romance #3404 in April
Make Believe Engagement by Day Leclaire

Harlequin Temptation #588 in May
Stranger in the Night by Roseanne Williams

Harlequin Superromance #695 in June
Married to a Stranger by Connie Bennett

Harlequin Historicals #324 in July
Dulcie's Gift by Ruth Langan

Visit Bride's Bay Resort each month wherever
Harlequin books are sold.

If you enjoyed this book by

RITA CLAY ESTRADA

Here's your chance to order more stories by one of
Harlequin's favorite authors:

Harlequin Temptation®

#25461	TWICE LOVED	$2.99	☐
#25574	THE COLONEL'S DAUGHTER	$2.99	☐
#25600	FORMS OF LOVE	$2.99 U.S.	☐
		$3.50 CAN.	☐
#25618	THE TWELVE GIFTS OF CHRISTMAS	$2.99 U.S.	☐
		$3.50 CAN.	☐

(limited quantities available on certain titles)

TOTAL AMOUNT	$
POSTAGE & HANDLING	$
($1.00 for one book, 50¢ for each additional)	
APPLICABLE TAXES*	$_____
TOTAL PAYABLE	$_____
(check or money order—please do not send cash)	

To order, complete this form and send it, along with a check or money order
for the total above, payable to Harlequin Books, to: **In the U.S.:** 3010 Walden
Avenue, P.O. Box 9047, Buffalo, NY 14269-9047; **In Canada:** P.O. Box 613,
Fort Erie, Ontario, L2A 5X3.

Name: _____

Address: _____ City: _____

State/Prov.: _____ Zip/Postal Code: _____

*New York residents remit applicable sales taxes.
Canadian residents remit applicable GST and provincial taxes.

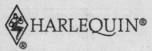

Look us up on-line at: http://www.romance.net

Mail Order Men—Satisfaction Guaranteed!

Texas Man—Tanner Jones

This rugged construction worker is six-feet tall, with brown hair and blue eyes. His ideal woman is one who values love, trust and honesty above possessions.

Tanner Jones seems to be the answer to Dori Fitzpatrick's prayers. Ever since her rich ex-husband took her five-year-old son away from her, Dori's been looking for a way to get little Jimmy back. And she needs a husband to do it—preferably one who works for a living. But Dori soon finds out there's more to Tanner than meets the eye.

#600 HOLDING OUT FOR A HERO
by Vicki Lewis Thompson

Available in August wherever
Harlequin books are sold.

HARLEQUIN®
Temptation

Look us up on-line at: http://www.romance.net

MMEN

You're About to
Become a
Privileged
Woman

Reap the rewards of fabulous free gifts and benefits with proofs-of-purchase from Harlequin and Silhouette books

Pages & Privileges™

It's our way of thanking you for buying our books at your favorite retail stores.

PROOF OF PURCHASE
HT-PP152
Offer expires October 31, 1996

**Harlequin and Silhouette—
the most privileged readers in the world!**

For more information about Harlequin and Silhouette's PAGES & PRIVILEGES program call the Pages & Privileges Benefits Desk: 1-503-794-2499

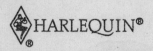

HARLEQUIN®

HT-PP152